This BOOK belongs to:

Credits:

Cover Art by Phatpuppy Creations
phatpuppyart.com
Cover design and art by Elizabeth Watasin

Cover model is Elizabeth Worth
www.modelmayhem.com/3122503
Custom Wardrobe Creation: Cavalyn Galano
www.facebook.com/CavalynDesign
Makeup/Hair: Nadya Rutman
www.bynadya.com
Photography: Teresa Yeh Photography
www.teresayeh.com

Typography by Tom Orzechowski and Lois Buhalis
www.serifsup.com

Editing by JoSelle Vanderhooft
www.joselle-vanderhooft.com

More Books
by
Elizabeth Watasin

The Dark Victorian: Risen

The Dark Victorian: Bones

Sundark: An Elle Black Penny Dread

Charm School Graphique, Vol 1-5

Charm School Digital, No 1-10

An A-Girl Studio book
published 2014 in the USA.

For additional information, please contact:
A-Girl Studio
P.O. Box 213, Burbank, CA 91503 U.S.A.
www.a-girlstudio.com

ISBN: 978-1-936622-22-1
Library of Congress Control Number: 2014918434
First paperback edition, 2014

❖

Ice Demon: A Dark Victorian Penny Dread

Volume 1

By
Elizabeth Watasin

A-GIRL STUDIO

CHAPTER ONE

"Thee, of stars."

Upon an icy quay in the Upper Pool of London, in the stretch of the Thames before London Bridge, a welcoming party waited before a row of carriages. Their gazes were fixed on the Lower Pool, searching the ships that slowly manoeuvred the choppy waters to dock or depart. White fog thickened above the river.

Mrs Rowden stood, rosy-cheeked and shivering, with her stately, older friend, Lady Baffin, both wearing muffs for their hands and scarves over their hats. A brass band abided behind them, the men bundled in wool coats. Each man carried an instrument—a cornet, trombone, horn, and tuba—in gloved hands. They hunched against the wind and stamped their feet for warmth.

"This unnatural cold we're having," Mrs Rowden said, and her breath clouded before her. "It shall be worse tonight when the ice fog settles. The worst in ages."

"Which is why I'm thankful the expedition comes home to-day," Lady Baffin said. "Winter is not the season for man nor beast in the unforgiving Arctic." She glanced at Mrs Rowden.

"You're nearly frozen, Genny dear. Wait in my carriage. It has a stove."

Genny turned to her. "While you stand alone here, Gertie? Oh no! We'll be back in our warm homes soon enough, I've a roaring fire waiting for my John!"

She and Lady Baffin returned their attention to the Thames and watched small ships sway against the wind. The vessels bobbed and slowly hazed from view as the fog rolled in.

"There!" Genny cried. "The SS *Terror*!"

She pointed to a thick ship with three masts that emerged from the fog bank, its sails furled. They watched its shape increase, the iron-plated hull frosted white.

"How snowbound the *Terror* looks in that fog, even as it moves!" Genny exclaimed. "It brings the Arctic with it!"

"Yet how happy the crew must be, to be home at last," Lady Baffin said warmly. "See how it tries to advance ahead of the sea smoke."

The *Terror* crept with the fog resting on its deck. It lumbered in the rolling waters, narrowly brushing the other vessels it passed. Ships' bells rang in warning.

"I cannot see the helm for the fog. The ship, it moves with bare steerageway," Genny said. "No power from its sails . . . no smoke from the steam engine. I wonder—*oh*!"

The *Terror* collided with a smaller vessel, sending it veering aside. It struck another with a loud *crack* to the boat's stern.

Genny watched with held breath as ships hastened out of the way, more bells ringing.

"If my John's at ship's wheel," Genny said, "or Captain Buck-amore—"

"They can't be faulted, dear. The propellers, they must be damaged," Lady Baffin said. "No steering can guide a ship that size without the propellers."

The ship drew closer, flanked by fog. Icicles hung from the yards. The loosely furled mainsail flapped its shredded cloth, and behind it, the ripped third sail flogged.

"I thought those were made of triple canvas?" Genny said.

"What a terrible ice storm they must have faced," Lady Baffin said.

Genny stood on her toes. A large man covered in thick furs and with a furred hood tight around his bearded face stood starboard. He gripped the frosted handrail with fur-mittened hands.

"Look there! Lord Baffin wears his great furs!" she cried. She turned to Lady Baffin. "What a giant figure of a man he makes!"

Lady Baffin nodded with a broad smile, a gloved hand to her throat. Genny tidied a stray lock of auburn hair come loose from the harsh wind.

"The ship will soon be here," Genny said. "The band should play!"

"Yes! Let us welcome him home." Lady Baffin turned to the band. "If you please, play the song I wish Lord Baffin to hear!"

The band nodded, doffed gloves, put lips to mouthpieces, and began the first sprightly notes of "The Lass That Loves a Sailor."

Lady Baffin turned back, beaming. Genny watched the *Terror* glide closer with Sir Baffin steady and still at the handrail. The frosted hull loomed.

"The refrain shall give them courage for these last yards!" she said.

In a clear soprano, she accompanied the band:

> "But the standing toast, that pleas'd the most,
> Was "The wind that blows, the ship that goes,
> And the lass that loves a sailor!""

Genny clapped in delight as the band played on. She looked closely at the approaching ship.

"Why does Sir Baffin not acknowledge us?" she said.

The iron hull came quickly upon them.

Genny grabbed Lady Baffin as the hull struck the quay with the tremendous sound of splintering wood and creaking timber. The waters surged and the *Terror* sank back. Sir Baffin tumbled headfirst over the handrail for the walk below. His fur-covered head and body struck the walk and shattered.

Shards of Sir Baffin slid on the icy quay and streaked the surface pink, the glistening pieces like frozen butcher slices. Genny screamed and the band members collided with each other. Amid the jostling panic, Lady Baffin stared. At her feet was the sharp fragment that contained the calm, grey eye and partial white face of her husband.

Genny dragged Lady Baffin away. Something else dropped from the ship and she cringed. But the male figure in the dark pea coat landed feet-first on the wrecked quay. He straightened, turned, and walked into the thickening fog.

"John?" she cried.

~✖~

Snow fell on a night-bound London.

Drifts grew and the ice fog descended, engulfing the city. Artifice, artificial ghost and agent of HRH's Secret Commission, flew down the streets and through slow-moving carriages, her pale, six-foot-two form transparent and glowing. She would have turned entirely invisible, but as her partner Jim had advised, it would better suit London if the city grew accustomed to her ghostly figure flying about. Barely a yard could be seen ahead of her, and she doubted even a lantern would have helped cut through the thick fog. The chilling wind did not disturb her hat or the long overcoat she wore over her broad-shouldered, slim-waisted body, but her skirts flapped, and Art could never explain why that happened when she was in her Fourth Dimensional state. She held her silver-headed, iron-wood walking stick to her and flew on through the last falling snowflakes, discerning which of the fog-ridden streets would lead her to the Pool of London.

She finally alighted on the damaged quay where a policeman in a heavy coat stood watch and warmed his hands before a can fire. She took solid form before her spectral transparency could alarm him and approached, giving a friendly greeting. He saw her, peered at her Secret Commission badge, and touched his helmet. She walked to a spot beside the moored ship and set her stick to the quay.

The SS *Terror*, she read upon the ship's thickly frosted forward end. She felt the bite of flying ice crystals on her face, and the weight of a small drift piling at her feet. The policeman hunched over his can.

Though this was her first winter since being resurrected by the Secret Commission, she recognised the uncommon chill of the night. A rare cold had fallen upon London. The mooring ropes were feathering with white rime ice, and Art was certain they were lengthening before her gaze. She hardened her muscles against the wind. If she stood long enough, platy ice crystals might grow upon her person.

She looked up at the *Terror*'s yards with their shredded furled sails, the scraps flapping. The large icicles that hung from them pointed long, glistening fingers down. Of the ships she'd flown past to find the *Terror*, she'd not seen one with so much ice already grown upon it.

Art heard the swift hooves of a horse and its hansom cab on the walk. The cab emerged from the thick fog, a blonde girl seated within. Nearly eighteen years of age, she carried a skull in a top hat in her gloved hand. Art's partner—the animated skull Jim Dastard—and their assistant, Delphia Bloom, had arrived.

Delphia hopped from the hansom cab, light of foot and with Jim in hand, the cold seemingly without effect on her youthful vigour, though she was bundled in a thick scarf and long coat, ice crystals sticking to her goggles' lenses. She removed them from her grey eyes and stored them on her riding hat. Art raised her stick in greeting and Jim hailed.

"Ho! Strongwoman! How does your perfect physique fare against winter's bilious, white breath? You could avoid the effects of this harrowing weather by ghosting, but no! Stout-hearted you stand!"

"Cold strengthens the body," Art said. "But this night is unduly trying, Jim. I was with the Friends, handing blankets and coats to those less fortunate when thee gave me signal to meet thee here. 'Twill be a harsh night for our poor."

"Your need for rescue, young Quaker, is commendable," Jim said. "Especially when it serves as personal recompense for all the violence your peaceful soul must enact whilst an agent of His Royal Highness's Secret Commission. England thanks you! But you can return to your shivering poor after we've viewed those already frozen."

"Sounds a strange, and rather gruesome, case, Art and sir," Delphia said. "Though all our cases are such. How can an entire body be transformed to mere fragile ice? I can see the blood on the walk where Sir Baffin's body is said to have smashed to pieces."

They looked down at the stains on the icy quay. The policeman threw more bits of coal into his fire.

"This night may freeze blood, and the wet air works to coat all with rime, but has thee noticed, Friends, that this ship is the only one with glaze ice upon the yards?" Art said. "And with hoarfrost on its hull, thick enough for a knife?"

"The *Terror* has retained its Arctic features, true. All the way back to London," Jim said as he and Delphia surveyed the vessel. "Curious. Let us board."

Art heard descending steps sound on the gangplank. A spectacled old man in a tall top hat and long coat hurried down, carrying his black bag. The lanky form of Sgt Barkley followed him.

"Zymotic disease," the doctor pronounced when he saw the agents' Secret Commission badges. He brushed past them. "Whether ingested, or passed on from fellow to fellow. The ship's doctor's notes are all frozen! I'll read them when they've thawed."

"Then the ship's doctor concluded the deaths are from disease?" Jim called after the departing man. The doctor made an impatient gesture.

"No!" he said. "But it must be. Good night to you!"

He hurried into a waiting carriage and slammed the door. As the carriage pulled away, the three turned to Barkley, who smiled and touched his bowler.

"Mr Dastard, Art, Miss Bloom. Think we all would like this night done and a warm meal in our bellies," he said. He hunched his shoulders in his coat. "Well, to it! The ship's the SS *Terror*, as you must know by now, and built and financed by the Royal Geographical Society. The purpose of the vessel, an Arctic expedition led by Sir Francis Baffin to gather polar magnetic readings."

He glanced up at the ship. "And somehow it sailed all the way there with eighty hearty men and returned with the same, all frozen. Don't know what more to tell you except you can see it for yourselves, once aboard. We've inspected it, top to bottom, and left all untouched. We'll remove bodies in the morning. Oh! And the *Times* journalist Miss Skycourt is aboard, with her sister—the Lady Helene—and an illustrator from *The Strand*."

Helia and Helene are here! Art thought. She had not seen Helia's penny-farthing on the quay and wondered which waiting carriage was theirs.

"Lady Helene!" Jim said. "An adventuress who can't resist a mystery. No doubt in the morning more of Sir Baffin's explorers' circle will want to tour the *Terror*."

"And I'll be here come morning to keep those hoity-toities out, unless they're earls or dukes," Barkley said cheerfully.

"This fearsome chill has kept even the most persistent of the journalists away. With the exception, of course, of a certain madwoman!"

At the mention of "madwoman", Art looked up at the ship. Helia Skycourt stood smiling and gaily waving at the handrail, as if the night weren't bitterly cold or the ship she stood on hadn't torn sails and frightful icicles. She wore a leather half-mask, red earmuffs, a long red scarf over her hat and around her neck, a red muff, and a small, hanging leather satchel by her side. Strands of her untidy, dark hair danced around her face. Art thought her leather gloves too thin for the weather.

After more pleasantries, Barkley bade them good night and strolled quickly for another waiting carriage. Art ghosted and sailed up the gangplank.

"Once onboard we might get relief from this wind and chilling fog," Delphia said, following. She mounted the plank with wide strides.

～

The *Terror*'s bleak deck, with its beating, ripped sails and growing white drifts was a dismal, algid meeting place. But Art only had eyes for Helia, who had brought out a tiny tin from her muff. Helia's blue eyes twinkled as Art hovered before her, and she opened it. Within was beeswax. She pulled off the glove of one hand and dabbed the wax.

"Please excuse my impropriety, Art," Helia said.

She applied the beeswax to her lips, rubbing her bottom lip with a bare finger. She then pressed her lips together to spread the wax while she donned her glove again. Art watched, fascinated.

"Miss Skycourt!" Jim exclaimed as Delphia boarded. Helia offered the tin of beeswax to her. Art took Jim in hand while Delphia curtsied and accepted the tin.

"It's good to see you again!" Jim continued. "No doubt you've scoured the ship already and concluded the mystery?"

Helia laughed. "Oh! How clever I'd be if that were true, Mr Dastard. Even my mad mind can't piece this puzzle."

"Miss Skycourt, you are less and less a madwoman with each passing night and day," Jim said as Delphia retrieved him.

Helia briefly touched her mask. She moved closer to Art and took her hand.

"I owe my present sanity to a very good woman," Helia said.

"It warms my heart to see my partner's silly grin from your words!" Jim said. "Makes the evils we face that much easier. Now, the police have been all over this ship and none fell victim to whatever killed the crew, eh? Let's see the handiwork of this possible zymotic killer."

Helia pointed down the creaking deck for the ship's wheel.

"Your first puzzle piece, Mr Dastard," she said. A white-frosted shape lay behind the wheel and binnacle, a drift of snow building against its side.

Jim activated his spectral glow and they approached. His light shone on the body of a burly, bearded man. He lay stiff and statue-like in his sea cap, guernsey, and oil coat, his gaze blank and his face and body gaping with dark cracks. His arm nearest the deck was nearly broken off. The shiny, pink meat of that arm hung from his shoulder like a chicken wing partially severed from the breast. Both his arms were spread wide and all the fingers snapped off.

"The captain," Jim said.

"Captain Buckamore," Helia said.

"Ah. Robust fellow. Looks like he was removed from ship's wheel after death, and unceremoniously. Perhaps the last of the living crew needed to steer?"

"The ship could not return to London without guidance, that's true, Mr Dastard," Helia said, nodding. "John Rowden might have done it; he was helmsman. His wife was on the quay when the *Terror* arrived. She thought she saw him jump off and walk away."

"Indeed? Hm. Watch your step, Delphia. The captain's fingers may be underfoot, though more likely rolled to other parts of the deck," Jim said.

"Fingers. Yes, sir," Delphia said stiffly.

Art grasped the ship's wheel. No frost was upon it. Sitting atop the compass's binnacle was a brass paraffin blow lamp, frozen fast to the surface. Art looked at the fuel can with its sturdy handle and angled burner head. The hand pump to pressurise the fuel was pulled up, as if the captain had been in the midst of priming the tool.

"Why does a blow lamp rest here, at the ready?" Art said.

Helia looked at it thoughtfully. "Such torches are used to thaw equipment or to seal pipes, Art," she said. "But yes, it is odd, resting here."

Delphia knelt by the stiff captain's body, ignoring his torn arm and maimed hands. She poked at one of his coat pockets with a pocketknife blade.

"Yes, something is in there!" Jim said. "You nearly have it, Bloom! Just don't cut the captain!"

"The pocket's been sliced open before, sir," Delphia said, concentrating on her work. "This cold only sealed it once more." She gave a triumphant sound, laid her blade aside, and reached into the slice.

"I was the one who first sliced it," Helia said. "You'll find a small bottle within. It's meant to keep a rolled sheet of paper dry."

"The rolled sheet is gone," Delphia said, holding up a slim, corked bottle.

"That is because I am thawing it," Helia admitted. "And it is still quite frozen." She patted her bosom.

"Very well! Return the bottle, Bloom, and we'll read Captain Buckamore's last words later! There's a ship's logbook we should consult."

Helia pointed towards the entryway of a deckhouse behind the wheel. "The navigation room is within, Mr Dastard. But you'll find it crowded with dead men, and the logbook perhaps somewhere in the frozen mess."

Delphia and Jim approached the deckhouse. Art turned to Helia and held out her hand.

"Hand me the paper, dear Helia, for I've the more generous bosom," she said.

Helia giggled and reached into her coat's chest front.

After accepting the iced paper and secreting it away within her bodice and coat, Art ghosted, and swept to the side of the deckhouse. She spied the porthole to the navigation room and wiped the frost from the glass. A man's face and hand appeared.

"Art?" Helia asked when Art gasped.

"I was only startled, Helia." Art swallowed. "'Tis . . . like looking at a tank in the Royal Aquarium."

"Yes . . . of drowned men."

Jim's spectral glow drifted about the room. The navigation room was frozen in midflurry; maps, instruments, and pencils upended and iced while in motion. So too were the four seamen within, their rough guernseys and dark trousers frosted white. They were a pressed mass with silent, screaming mouths, scrambling to escape something behind them. The foremost man's eyes were closed, his eyelashes frosted white. His fingers pushed against the portal's glass.

"'Tisn't zymotic disease that took thee," Art said quietly to the men. "Thee were hale and hearty, and died fleeing."

She touched the window where the frozen man's fingers pressed and closed her eyes.

"Art! Oh, sorry, didn't mean to interrupt."

Art turned and saw Delphia and Jim with Helia.

"Bloom and I entered the navigation room and saw a blow lamp dropped within, probably by the unfortunate men. It left quite a burn on the floor. We'll now descend for the sick bay."

"The doctor and his notes will be there, Mr Dastard," Helia said. "Frozen to his surgery table. As well as the remains of a man he was examining. Sick bay is fore of the ship, one deck below."

"Proceed ahead, Jim and Delphia, I will join thee," Art bade.

The two left, and Art dropped to the deck, solidifying.

"More such deaths wait below, do they not, Helia?" she said soberly.

"They do. It shall be like waxworks, Art. Gruesome in their finality."

Art took one of Helia's cold, gloved hands and rubbed it.

"As way opens," she said.

They entered the deckhouse together.

Helia climbed the ladder down while Art descended with her as a ghost. Finding the ship's entryways small for a woman of her height, Art decided not to test her body's breadth against the narrow ladders. The passageway was equally narrow and nearly pitch-dark. Deck prisms glowed above, faintly capturing the outside light and reflecting it to below. Helia moved down the rungs for the next deck, her breath white puffs in the air. When Art joined her, Helia lit a short candle stored in a portable tin with a hinged lid and stem handle, the length of a clay pipe. Its light added to Art's own spectral glow, and Art was relieved to not spy more frightened, frozen men revealed in the blackness.

"Where is thy adventuress sister in this frigid darkness?" Art asked.

"Studying the bones of this ship, I suspect," Helia said. She looked up at Art, her bright eyes shining. "How beautiful you look tonight. This is the first time I've seen you in one of Lottie's fetchingly designed coats."

"I ask pardon of this ship's dead seamen that I should indulge in my own admiration of thee," Art said. "For thee is even more beautiful. Especially while wearing cunning earmuffs. Might I beg a kiss?"

Helia rose on tiptoe to oblige. She held the candle away as they kissed. Art smiled when they parted.

"I kiss thee for love of thee, and not for information. Helene is not just here for admiration of a modern ship, is she?"

"No, Art, that's why I led you farther down, so that Mr Dastard might not overhear. Sir Baffin found something on his last Arctic expedition. He had this trip financed in order to retrieve it, and he needed to do so before winter set. I'm not certain he knew exactly what he found, and we still don't know what that discovery is, but while inebriated at a fellow explorer's dinner party, he boasted of it to a friend."

"The friend being Helene?"

"Not quite, though they are acquaintances. It was more that Helene overheard the conversation. What was said was enough to warrant her attention. We intended to approach Sir Baffin on his return, but then . . . this."

"The deaths," Art said.

"Yes. This is very unexpected. What I've shared with you of Sir Baffin's true mission, you and Mr Dastard would have concluded by the evidence aboard. Sir Baffin's quarters told Helene and me that much. But because of Helene's position, we could not tell you directly."

"Yet thee did," Art said, smiling.

"We love you," Helia whispered.

They kissed again. Art would have liked to kiss more but the ship's chill was sinking into her bones and Helia was shivering in her embrace.

"I've one more place to investigate, and it's the hold," Helia said. Art heard Delphia descend the ladder at the other end of the passageway, Jim's voice giving encouragement.

"I should rejoin Jim," Art said reluctantly. "Thee should wait for us."

Helia shook her head. "Don't worry, dear. None are aboard

but us and the dead."

She departed, and her quick feet gained the ladder for below, the handle of the candle held in her teeth. Art switched to ghost form, floated down the passageway, stopped, then solidified. She saw a bobbing light along with Jim's spectral glow and heard a woman's quiet, authoritative voice. She recognised the speaker: Helene, twin sister to Helia and heir to the Skycourt earldom and airship industry. Her trim, black-clad figure strolled down the passageway with Delphia and Jim following. She carried a policeman's handheld lantern. She spotted Art as she spoke.

"This ship is privately built, an achievement of modernity, but has a solidity worthy of service to the Royal Navy. These are double-thick decks," she said, "and are braced fore and aft with oak beams. It is iron-hulled and has a keel sheathed in the thickest copper. Triple-strength canvas was used for the sails. It's disappointing that they didn't last longer. But there's no question the *Terror* would have survived a return from the Arctic, even with the death of nearly all eighty of its men."

"'Nearly', Helene?" Art said. "How many men remaining would such a great ship need?"

Helene stopped before her and smiled, her spectacles glinting. The dark of the passageway could not diminish her keen, blue-eyed regard.

"Hello, Art. It appears only one man was needed, even without sails and engine. The dead men have been counted. Someone had to navigate the ship back to London, and that person was John Rowden, the *Terror*'s helmsman."

"So much thee knows of this vessel, Helene. Helia said thee likes ships. Both of air and sea."

Art looked Helene over. Helene had complemented the austere long, black coat over her black skirts with black gloves, blue scarf, furred grey earmuffs, and her black tricorne. Her lips glistened with beeswax. Art wondered what weapons she was hiding on her trim figure.

"And those under the sea," Helene said. "Art, stop looking at my pockets. I haven't treats."

Art tried not to blush. "Then I needn't perform a trick for thee."

She heard Jim chuckle while Helene raised an eyebrow.

"Back to the matter at hand," Jim said with humour.

"Yes, of course. As Helia told you, Genevieve Rowden said she saw her husband jump from the ship. If so, what do you think left him alive and all these men dead?"

"'Twasn't zymotic disease," Art said.

"I agree."

"Art," Jim said, "Lady Helene has already toured most of the ship. We're behind in our investigation. Onward to the hold. Delphia and Lady Helene can squeeze by your impressive size, but better you turn around and lead, if you would."

Art did so, walking down the passageway for the ladder. Helia quickly emerged from the dark below, the stem of her candle between her teeth and her boots clicking on each wooden rung. Her eyes twinkled up at Art as she swiftly stepped over the lip, gripping the rails. She removed her candle from her mouth.

"They'd had quite the conflagration," she said to the group. "The engine room and boiler are thoroughly iced, including the men. Aldosia has already found her way there."

Then she squeezed by Art, Helene, Delphia, and Jim and disappeared down the passageway.

"Miss Skycourt is ahead of the game!" Jim said. "To below!"

Art dropped down into the lower deck as a ghost while the others followed.

CHAPTER TWO

When Art reached the bottom, she drifted in the direction she thought was the fore of the ship. In truth, she knew nothing of ships, so she was uncertain where the hold would be. Delphia hopped down into the darkness, Jim's glowing presence in her hand.

"Art, I believe it's the other way," he said.

"Are you certain, sir? Aft?" Delphia said.

"Er, which way is which again?"

"Well, fore is where Art is going. Aft is—"

Delphia and Jim screamed.

Art rushed behind Delphia and solidified, stick in hand. She reached up the ladder and stilled Helene's descending foot at the ankle. Jim's glow revealed a seaman covered in frost. He lunged for Delphia while in frozen flight, his ice-glazed eyes wide and his mouth open as if to speak. Several of his fingers had broken off. Art noticed the patterned ribbing of his jumper and wondered what island or coastal family had knitted the distinct design.

Art released Helene's ankle, and Helene jumped the rest of the way down. She squeezed next to Art to raise her lantern. Her light revealed more men behind the reaching one, all in the midst of fleeing something behind them. In the very back, Art spied one figure who had fallen against the wall after turning to ice, his head broken off at the neck by the impact. But his detached head had frozen to the wall, as if from enduring a continuous freezing.

Art pointed at the grotesque figure with her stick's handle, and Helene touched Art's bicep in acknowledgement.

"Yes," she said, her voice low. "Something chose to press the attack."

"Ahem." Jim cleared his throat. "You rarely scream in so girl-ish a fashion, Delphia."

"Sir, I believe you screamed louder than I did."

"Yes, well. He can't do anything to us—he and the rest. They're mere statues now," Jim said. "Uh. Onward."

"Fore or aft, sir?" Delphia asked.

Helene squeezed by Art and proceeded down the passageway free of frozen men.

"Fore. Those men are from the engine room," she said, her lantern's light leading.

Art allowed Delphia and Jim to proceed her, more to reassure them that she would watch the procession's rear. She paused and considered the option of swiftly investigating the engine room herself. She heard someone shuffle in the passageway and looked back. A short, plump woman in a heavy coat, furred hat, and with thick spectacles held the rails of the ladder as she carefully stepped up. Like Helia, she wore thin gloves and a leather satchel as well as a muff on strings. Between her teeth, she clenched her own candle tin.

Aldosia Stropps, Art thought, *the illustrator for the* Strand.

Aldosia, as was her habit, completely ignored Art's spectral presence and continued determinedly up. Art concluded that since Aldosia had emerged from the engine room unscathed, that area was no longer a danger. Art continued down the pas-sageway.

～

The hold showed an impressive black burn, from floor to high ceiling, with moist soot coating storage barrels and crates. Black particles still drifted, and both Delphia and Helene protected their noses and mouths with their scarves. The place smelled of old smoke and brine. A burnt steam engine sat in a pool of dirty ice and water, its steam pipe broken. A shattered gauge's black face jutted out. A set of twisted tubes from the machine led to a charred, long wood box with thick sides. It lay awkwardly on its side, the blackened door ajar. Water pooled from it. Art reached out with the end of her stick and scraped the soot off the surface of a battered, iron storage can. The label read: *Sulphuric Ether*.

"An impressive fire," Jim said.

"Indeed, for it was fuelled," Helene said as she shone her lamp on the steam engine. "I shall intuit a very simple scenario: a man was careless with the sulphuric ether meant to cool the refrigeration machine, resulting in its combustion."

"Thee refers to this ice box," Art said. She used her stick's handle to hook the heavy door and lift it. The thick walls within held nothing but a slag of ice.

"Yes. A mechanical icebox, Art. The engine operates the condenser for the ether, which cools the brine circulated in the box. Ether vapour is easily ignitable."

"An Arctic vessel with *cold* storage. Ha! 'Magnetic readings', my non-existent foot," Jim said. "Baffin was after more than that when he had this expedition funded. And once he retrieved it, well, what did he pack in there? Frozen treasure? The narrow block seems the size of a coffin."

"One for a small woman," Delphia said. She happened to glance at Helene, then averted her gaze.

"Aye, Helene could fit it," Art said.

"I cannot," Helene said. "I'm taller than that."

"Aye," Art said. "Helia is taller."

Art ignored Helene's incensed look.

"Well, whatever was in it melted away. Or was absconded with. That icebox, there," Jim said. "With the handprints in the soot as if it had been recently opened. I wonder—"

"Shall I open it, sir?" Delphia reached for the unlocked lid of a large icebox similar to those used in manor kitchens. She lifted it, and a man's face in pieces looked up at her. More of his body shards lay in the stained, packed ice. Delphia dropped the lid.

"So that's where some of the men went," Jim said.

"Yes, sir," Delphia said in a tight voice. "After they'd been dropped, and such."

"Well! Let us travel from this place of death to another."

Helene led the way out with Delphia following and Art in the rear. As Delphia stepped out the entryway, she glanced back at the burnt hold. "And yet . . . unlike most of the ship, Art and sir, this death-place bears no frost."

Art touched her stick's handle to her chin and contemplated that.

They left the hold, squeezed by the frozen men they'd encountered before, and made their way aft for the engine room. As Helia had described, the place was blanketed in frost that sparkled before Helene's lantern, the long teeth of glaze ice glistening from the pipes overhead. Some icicles had fallen to the metal grating of the walk, and when Art's step echoed on the metal, more fell and tinkled on impact. The black furnace sat dead, two frozen men with shovels staring blankly at the visitors' intrusion. A man in braces and a Crimean shirt stood with chin raised before the brass engine order telegraph, his eyes shut as if in prayer or contemplation. One end of his thick moustache had snapped off. Art turned from him and looked at a shelf illuminated by Helene's lantern. The space was empty but for a dented paraffin can.

"Not one blow lamp left in stores," Helene said.

～

When they ascended to the upper deck, Art floated ahead and heard typewriter keys clack. She followed the sound down the passageway to a small galley with glimmering walls, benches, and tables, sheathed in thin ice. Frosted men dressed in shirts of wool or serge sat silent and still in the shadows, their tins of food before them. A boy in wool pea jacket and cap held a spoon to his open mouth. Helia typed on a compact folding typewriter that stood on an ice-covered countertop. She danced a little as she typed and exhaled white puffs of mist. Her satchel hung open at her side, revealing the moulded compartment where the folded typewriter had resided. Aldosia stood in full view of the whitened room sketching rapidly on a small board that held clipped paper. Both women's tiny candles lit the galley, and if the still men could be seen as sleeping, Art could nearly take the scene for serene. The place seemed more frigid than any room she'd encountered on the ship. She nearly wondered why the two were working there, in such glacial surroundings, but she didn't have to. In that galley sat the true story of the *Terror*, of innocent men oblivious to the death that took them.

Helia looked up and stopped typing. "What do you see, dear?" she asked.

"There was no strife here, Helia. These men were caught unaware," Art said. "Even the little boy did not look to the door. What walked in and did this might have been known to them."

Helia nodded. She turned back to her typewriter and typed more. Delphia and Jim stepped into the galley.

"Ah, the *Strand* illustrator who needs only see a thing once and can draw it all! Miss Aldosia Stropps, hello! Miss Stropps is an exceptional draftswoman, Bloom. And has a malady of the mouth to her brain," Jim added *sotto voce*.

"Satan," Aldosia said.

"What?" Delphia said.

"Satan's teats!" Aldosia said as she drew. "Teats, teats!"

"Teats," Art repeated thoughtfully.

"Dis's teats!" Aldosia said.

Helia stopped typing, then exclaimed.

"Why, yes, Aldosia! How like hell's ninth circle this is!"

"Canto XXXIV," Delphia said. "'That from him issued three winds, wherewith Cocytus was made frozen.'"

"Hm, yes. I prefer when you quote medical journals, Bloom," Jim said. "Never cared for *Inferno*. Let's follow the spoor of this Satan, then, and see what else his beating wings have frozen. A pleasure to see you, Miss Stropps!"

Delphia stepped out of the galley with Jim.

"Testicles," Aldosia muttered.

She pushed at the bridge of her spectacles, then continued to draw. Art stepped closer to see if she were really illustrating a glacial circle of hell. On the paper was an exact representation of the galley, including the tins of food and frozen boy and men. Aldosia moved her pencil to a corner of her paper and drew a cartoon of Art peering down at her.

"Ha-ha," Art said. "My bosom. Thee draws it large."

"Art," Helene said.

She turned. Helene stood right behind her. Aldosia gathered her things and squeezed past them as she left the galley. Helia folded her portable typewriter, picked it up, and followed. At the doorway, she looked back at Art and smiled.

"I've toured the ship from stem to stern and found only Sir Baffin's quarters of interest," Helene said, drawing Art's attention back to her again. "Come take a look."

～

Jim and Delphia were already within Sir Baffin's quarters, Jim's glow illuminating the small space. Art entered and went directly to the desk. Sir Baffin's iced journal lay open, the frost carefully brushed away by someone's hand. Before she could read it, Jim exclaimed, "These are peculiar."

Art turned to see. Delphia had, in the midst of searching the cot, pulled up the bedding. Between the mattress and padding, bright metal fragments as big as Art's palm sat. Their edges were dark, as if burnt. A pistol sat beside them.

"Such thick fragments . . . like for walls," Delphia said, picking one up. The metal reflected light on its iridescent surface, creating a change of colours. "What an odd material."

"They're very little pieces," Jim said. "And no larger ones were in the hold. Evidence, perhaps, of another moment of destruction. Is Lady Helene here?"

"I am," Helene said from the entryway.

Delphia turned so that Jim could look upon her.

"Do you recognise such singular metal, M'Lady? Perhaps as something used in the construction of one of your airships?"

"I do not, Mr Dastard. It's certainly a queer find."

Art watched the interaction between Helene and Jim, her stick's silver handle to her chin. She turned in thought and silently read the page opened in Sir Baffin's frozen journal:

> —SHE, in turn, cannot fathom us. Can she hear my words? Is she naught but a simple scorpion? But what scorpion dares to speak, as she has tried to do? I can give her a home! Just like the one she had known. She must be made to understand that what happened was an accident, back in the hold. I will not let the ship turn back. I will—

The entry ended, the pen having blotted the paper. Art touched the edge of the page. Thoroughly iced, it would not turn.

"This 'she'," Art said.

"Yes," Jim said. "We'd read that. Near akin to feverish ranting. Does he refer to the *Terror*?"

"Yet what 'home' does Sir Baffin wish to give the *Terror*?" Delphia asked. "I would also not describe such a robust ship as a scorpion."

"Nay," Art said. "The 'she' he describes was that one held in the wee ice coffin."

"In the refrigeration machine?" Jim said. "An ice woman, then? Extraordinary. Then where is she, if John Rowden is gone?"

"Our presence aboard did not tempt this . . . female to emerge. It can be concluded that she is also gone," Helene agreed.

Art ghosted and flew out of the room.

She rose swiftly through the decks until she reached the deckhouse. There, Helia knelt in the shelter of the passageway and typed. Art solidified, relieved that she was safe. Helia smiled, folded her typewriter, and rose.

"Thee should not remain longer on this death ship," Art said, approaching. "'Tis too bitter for the living." She unbuttoned her coat and wrapped Helia in the folds. Helia pressed her cold face to Art's bodice front and hugged her.

"Oh! You are warm," she sighed. "And so solid!"

"I've steeled my muscles 'gainst the cold," Art said. "'Tis protection!"

"And your bosom?"

"That retains its buoyancy."

Helia giggled against her chest, and they embraced. Back in Sir Baffin's quarters, Art knew Helene had been correct about the creature; they'd been onboard long enough to be attacked. It was long gone. She was nearly lost in the pleasure of warming Helia until she remembered something.

"The captain's note," Art said.

Helia looked up, smiling. She reached into Art's bodice, pulled the paper out, turned around in Art's arms, and brought her hands out from the coat folds. The paper, torn from a note-

book, unrolled without trouble. The words were scrawled in
thick pencil. They read it together.

> *All men dead but for Baffin and I, and he awaits
> its coming—North Wind, Freya, demon—what have
> you, and damn you, Baffin, you coward! Accepting its
> punishment will not right his sins. If I cannot sink the
> ship, then beware, you who reads this. My soul to God.
> Forgive us for what we took from its home.*

Art held the note while Helia copied it to her notebook.

"His last words, given in wrath," Art said thoughtfully.

"He hadn't time for pious reflection, perhaps," Helia said.

"'Demon'," Art repeated. She let the paper roll up and
hugged Helia to her.

When Art heard Delphia, Jim, and Helene climb the ladder
for the deckhouse, they parted. Art rebuttoned her coat and
Helia straightened the lapels.

". . . and we have her training in gymnastics," Jim said as
Delphia stepped foot in the passageway. "Aerobatics, yo-gah,
tightrope walking, horseback riding, target shooting—"

"I see! I recall that a circus cowboy taught Delphia tricks
of his trade," Helene said when she emerged from the ladder.
"Can you shoot targets from horseback, Delphia?"

"Well, I am practicing," Delphia said, sounding flustered.

"You will always be in practice," Helene said. "It is the dif-
ference between dying and surviving. And Delphia. I can see
the silhouette of your cudgel beneath your coat. Learn to hide
it better."

"Friends," Art gently interrupted. She held up Captain
Buckamore's rolled paper.

While the three read the note, Helia stepped out of the deckhouse, and Art followed, relieved to leave the presence of death
at last. They crossed the deck for the handrail, and Art saw

Aldosia below on the ruined quay, standing by the policeman's fire and drawing on her rustling paper. The thick fog rolled in the dark around her. Helia moved for the gangplank, but Art paused and looked behind. Helene walked towards them, the biting wind sending her coat ends flapping.

Art held out her hand for Helene, who looked startled.

"Well, if you insist," Helene said gruffly.

Art helped both women to the gangplank, then followed them down.

"Satan beats his wings," Helia said, muffled by her scarf.

Art walked close, shielding them both from the wind.

When they reached the quay, Aldosia ceased drawing and followed them to the wagons and carts stored next to the buildings. Helene kicked at drifts that had gathered beneath the large wheels of a canvas-covered vehicle.

"Now we must be off," she announced.

She unfastened the ropes securing the canvas and pulled back the cloth. Beneath was one of Perseus Kingdom's electric, horseless buggies. It had a stuffed, leather high seat for two with a steering tiller and a small tray in back. Aldosia clambered over the lip of the tray and fell into the bed while Art hurried to Helia's side to help her step in. Once Helia was seated within, she and Aldosia covered themselves with the canvas, their backs to the high seat Helene leapt into. She lit the vehicle's lamps, and Art heard the keys of Helia's portable typewriter clatter beneath the canvas.

"Love, love, love!" Helia said happily.

She pulled out the sheet of paper she had typed and gave it to Art. Art kissed her gloved hand. She folded the note and tucked it into her bodice.

"I've no gift of poetic sweet nothings, Art, therefore I'll only wish you good night," Helene said.

She was turned in the seat, her hat low over her spectacles and her scarf to her chin. Art thought she could be holding the reins to a team of wild horses and would still look collected.

"Helene, good night. I love thee too. When we meet again, I'll have a treat for thee in my pocket."

Helene gave her an incredulous look and blushed. Art grinned. Helia resumed typing while Aldosia drew in her sketchbook, and Helene turned her attention to the quay. She released the handbrake. Art stepped back as the buggy jumped forwards and silently accelerated. Helia blew Art a kiss before the fog enveloped them.

Art hugged her stick and bounced about on her toes.

"Art, you've such a funny dance when Miss Skycourt blows you kisses," Jim said as he and Delphia joined her. "Brr! What a night! Mrs Rowden is who we should speak to next, but like most humans during these darkest hours, she'll be tucked in bed. Bloom! Now you're dancing!"

"Only to fight the chill, sir!" Delphia said as she hopped about.

"'Tis a trying night upon the body," Art said. "Delphia should also be in a warm bed. We will catch the man, but perhaps Mrs Rowden's visit can wait 'til morning."

"It's decided! I may be a mere skull, but my teeth are chattering! We spectres and one squire should be away! Delphia, when you're ready!"

"Aye, sir," Delphia said. She secured her hat, brought down her goggles, and firmly wrapped her scarf around her nose and mouth. Art bent and offered a cupped hand. Delphia stepped into it, seated herself on one of Art's shoulders, and tucked Jim into her arm. She then took firm hold of Art's other shoulder. Art rose, holding Delphia's legs, and hefted her stick.

"Ready!" Delphia said.

Art ran down the quay for Whitechapel and disappeared into the fog.

CHAPTER THREE

Several miles away, Genny Rowden's carriage rolled down Cheapside and turned down a side street, the driver slowing his horse to a more cautious pace in the fog. Genny wearily considered leaving the carriage and walking since she was so near home, then decided against it. She would only endure more chill outside in the icy air and wet drifts building on the streets. The bells of St Mary-le-Bow rang the hour.

Much earlier that dreadful day, she'd told the police and the one journalist who'd come to the wrecked quay of what she'd witnessed, including the escape of the man she thought might be her husband. On accompanying her distraught friend Gertrude back to the Baffins' residence, she found Gertrude's doctor, a very self-important middle-aged man, already there. He interviewed her as well and seemed to dismiss all of what she'd seen as imaginings brought on by hysteria. True, witnessing Sir Baffin's horrifying shattering had been shocking, but she was a woman of London and had experienced the Devil Dogs' deadly invasion and the Living Gargoyle flying about with snatched children. Gertrude was the grieving wife with the husband currently in little pieces, not she.

However, when Gertrude was rendered unconscious at last

with prescribed laudanum, Genny thought some of the tincture might have been slipped into the bitter tea the doctor made her drink. She ended up heavily drowsy due to "the excitements of the day", as the doctor put it, and succumbed. She'd had to remain at the Baffins' home, sleeping for hours when all she'd wanted was to go home. Perhaps the staff had also made her comfortable so she could be present when their hysterical mistress finally revived. Once Genny awoke, she thought otherwise and promptly left by carriage. A pressing concern needed addressing, one that, the longer it remained unanswered, might drive her frantic enough for laudanum's oblivion.

She mused over and over again on what had happened at the quay: did she truly see John jump from the *Terror*? She'd thought it was he before even learning from the police that all the crew had died and he alone was counted missing from those onboard. Therefore, she doubted she had conjured seeing him from a grief-stricken need to have him safe. And if what she'd seen were true, then she needed to go home. For if John were not there, she would have to think next on where he might be.

The carriage finally stopped before her residence.

"Here we are, ma'am," the driver called down, and her carriage door opened.

"Thank you, driver," Genny said as she stepped out into the freezing air. She reached up in the dark and paid him. "And a very good night to you."

He touched his brim. As the carriage rolled away into the fog, taking the pale light of its gas lamps with it, Genny hurried for her front door.

She had a live-in maid who would let her in, a much older widow who had needed shelter and employment, and Genny was only too happy to give it to her. But after knocking awhile on her own front door, Genny questioned her own generosity regarding penniless widows. She suspected that Mrs Farney sometimes tippled, and she hoped, after everything she'd gone through that day, that her maid had not indulged in a little something to help her sleep. At last she gave up knocking and considered her parlour bay windows by the front door. Stepping down into a drift, she inspected them. The plated glass was frosted, and ice had formed in the seams. She gave a frustrated sound at the extent to which thick ice had sealed the windows.

"This will need a blow lamp to thaw," she muttered.

She judged that one window had less ice than the rest and took hold of its handle. Mrs Farney often neglected latching the windows at night, and it had become Genny's responsibility, which she knew hadn't been done after the parlour's morning airing in preparation for John's return. Some in her present society would be appalled at what she was about to do, for a lady never exerted herself. But she and John had elevated themselves from humbler beginnings, and perfecting her respectability had never concerned her greatly. It was very late; it was too cold for her to remain outside another second; and no one except perhaps the policeman on patrol was about to see her burgle her own home. Genny gritted her teeth and with all her strength, pulled the window open. A blast of freezing air met her, snatching her breath away.

She pressed her scarf to her nose and mouth and clambered over the sill. The air was as frigid as when her child self had fallen into the winter Thames. Frost came away on her gloved hands.

Had snow come in? she thought in bewilderment.

Her foot slipped on the slick wood floor. All about her in the darkness, her parlour glimmered. Everything was sheathed in ice.

She saw the dark figure of her maid standing near the shut door.

"Mrs Farney!" she called.

Another shape stood in the darkness, tall and male. She knew the pea coat and profile.

"*John?*" Genny shouted.

Thin, blue smoke issued from his pale lips and trailed into the shadows behind him. Genny saw something blue shimmer in the darkness, and a strange, gelatinous cloud emerged, attached to the trail. It glittered with ice flakes that winked and flashed, drifting around John to finally coalesce into a jelly body, curvaceous and female. Limbless, it slowly whirled, the tiny crystals within tumbling and flashing. The flickering ice flints showered down, then rose. It danced in Genny's parlour.

"John?" Genny cried. "What is that?"

The jelly cloud stilled. Somehow, it looked at her. Then it rushed between John's parted lips, disappearing completely within him.

Genny stifled a scream and tried to step forwards, slipping on the ice instead.

"What is happening?" she demanded.

John turned and faced her. She saw no recognition in his wide, glassy eyes.

"*Hhhome,*" he whispered, his voice high and strange.

"W-who is that inside my John?" she cried.

His mouth opened. A whirl of white and ice particles left his parted lips. Genny backpedalled as the whirlwind swiftly grew. Her legs hit the sill.

She turned and fell out the window.

~

John stepped slowly to the open window. He took hold of the frame and climbed out, finding no one there. His foot landed on a woman's hat. The great fog all around was spun with moisture and ice, thick and edible. He walked out upon the dark street; he kept walking. He held his hands high as if to reach for the whitened air, but no matter how far he walked, he could get no nearer to the rolling fog. He opened his arms and mouth wide. The clouds billowed and swirled, slicking the street and frosting the buildings, then it rushed into his mouth.

"'Ere—what, what are yer doing?" a policeman exclaimed, approaching.

He raised his lantern. John paused; the brightness of the lantern marred the beauty of the gelid darkness. He turned and exhaled, emitting a rushing fog of glittering crystals that brushed the man.

"*Argh!*" the policeman screamed. He recoiled and fled.

The policeman stumbled stiffly down the dark street for St Mary-le-Bow, his lantern's light bobbing. John blew, and the whirling fog grew, engulfing the man. The lantern snuffed out, and the policeman halted in midrun, keeling over the church's low hedge that was piled with drift. He struck the ground with a loud *crack* and broke in two.

At dawn, a thickly obscured London stirred. Art stood on a street corner near the Rowden residence, Jim in hand. Her spectral paleness was nearly indistinguishable from their frosted surroundings as delivery carts and costermonger barrows rolled by them in the dimness. The street they stood on appeared middle class, one of the few that sat between lanes of Cheapside shops, working-class streets, and the warrens of tenements. Jim pointed out that Charlotte Thackery, Art's dressmaker and outfitter, was only a brief walk from their location. A red-cheeked boy in a cap and long scarf cleared steps and walkways of drifts with his shovel while a coal horse and its heavy cart trundled into view, only to be swallowed by fog again. Jim smoked cigarettes, wondered where the newsboys were so he could read Helia's account of the *Terror*, and brought up the subject of Art's lady loves, the Skycourt twins.

"Art, your polyaphroditic courtship is advancing rather slowly. My old partner Dex would have married five women by now."

"Thee told me he had three wives!"

"Oh. Or was that Billy? Who didn't have time to marry his sweethearts, as a train ate him. Poor wretch. Have you need of more love counsel? I've a nice collection of books on the art of—"

"No, no," Art hastily said. "'Tis a delicate matter, Jim, that no book may have answers for. My death's circumstances do complicate my situation. But be assured. Win them, I shall."

With her partner thus placated, Art chose to describe the rooms and basements she'd visited in Whitechapel that night, filled with freezing poor.

"After erecting one fire," she said, "I returned, and an evil fellow had stomped upon it! For he wanted none to benefit of warmth, only because he were landlord and forbade it. Thus, I said to him, 'Would thee have these deaths upon thy conscience and soul? Would thee like it if I came to thy home and stomped on thy fire—'"

"Yes, yes," Jim interrupted. "And then you took a carriageful of the wretched basement dwellers and dumped them before the fire in his own drawing room, yes?"

"'Twas similar to that."

"Art, let's stop talking about the poor. I'm tired of hearing about our flea-bitten unfortunates. Yes, they suffer, and yes, they die. I am sorry for their lot, but I'd like to hear you talk about something cheery for once. Like all your lady-wooing."

"Thee asked me how my night was, Jim, and as we creatures have need for little sleep, I left the Vesta to lend aid. Thee may indulge in thy frivolities, smoking cigars and spending thy coin on watching women copulate with each other, but I demand nothing more of thee than thee lend sympathetic ear to my—"

"Yes, yes! Arrrgh! Good God, Art, I'll give thee alms, all right? So that you may set unlawful fires for your orphaned, widowed, shoeless, toothless, starving veterans! Just please stop talking about them!"

"Thee is a good man," Art said, smiling.

"Only because you make me suffer so, moral pest!" Jim said. He swallowed the last of his cigarette. "Ah! Relief! Bloom is finally here, ready with her quick mind and feet!"

A hansom cab arrived, bearing Delphia. She swiftly alighted and paid the driver. When she approached the two, buried in her scarf, her lowered brim did not hide the dark shadows beneath her eyes.

"You look terrible, Bloom!" Jim said.

"How fares your family, Delphia?" Art asked.

"It was a difficult night, Art and sir," Delphia said. "But all us Blooms emerged unscathed."

"You have a stove, don't you, Delphia?" Jim asked, clearly dismayed. "I know last night was the coldest London had ever seen but—the little ones haven't taken ill, have they?"

"Thee might give alms to the child," Art said coolly. "That might bandage the problems of her standing."

"Bloom here is a proud member of the working class! Stop being bitter about your huddled masses, Art." He swivelled in Art's hand. "Don't worry, Bloom. I'll provide your family with more coal."

"I and my family thank you, sir. I am not so proud to refuse such generous aid. This morning, I purchased hot coffee all around," Delphia said cheerfully. "We Blooms shall not succumb to Father Winter!"

"Brave lass!" Jim praised and hopped into the gloved hands Delphia held out to him. "To the Rowden residence!" he cried.

～

Art rapped on the door with the handle of her stick and waited. Though it was very early still, she and Jim were not above rousing humans from their warm beds. Delphia hopped up and down on the steps behind her.

"Such a chill on this spot," she said. "Almost like something's walked over my grave."

"Why is that window over there ajar on such a morning?" Jim remarked, referring to the ground-floor bay windows.

Art swiftly ghosted. She passed through the door and through the hallway wall leading into the room with the open window. Even in ghost form, the chill touched her. The parlour was crystallised, its drapes, furnishings, and knickknacks sheathed in glimmering ice. Art stared at the silent and still maid, who stared back. The frosted woman stood twisted on her heel for the door. Art heard a bump on the windowsill and turned. Delphia climbed through the open window with Jim. She also held a woman's hat, and carefully stepped down to the iced floor.

"Fie," Jim said soberly. "We're too late."

Art ghosted out into the hall. She flew into every room, armoire, closet, chest, beneath the beds, and then into the basement of the building, finding neither frozen body nor a hiding person.

"Mrs Rowden is not here," she said when she rejoined Jim and Delphia in the parlour.

"We believe this hat we found outside might be hers. No doubt, her husband was here," Jim said. "Look at this place. And that poor woman, who must have let her employer in."

"She thought to flee," Delphia said, staring at the frozen maid.

"I'd like to think, Delphia, that you would have fled faster," Jim said.

"The very walls are frozen," Art said, "and the chandelier weeps glaze ice. On the ship, we could excuse such evidence for Arctic remnants. 'Tis not so. Something entered here and willed this environment."

"Yet why?" Jim asked. "Why create this tiny, frozen horror-land, even insidiously colder than outside? We stand in a perfect pocket of Niflheim, just like the ship's galley."

"Indeed, sir. Perfect for frost giants from Jotunheim," Delphia solemnly said.

She and Jim departed by the window while Art ghosted into the street. As Jim had noted, the cold seemed less intense outside.

"The parlour door was still frozen shut, the maid blocking it. Therefore John Rowden left by the window," Jim said. "Now where would he go to?"

"He came home. And he is a seaman," Art said.

"Perhaps to the pub?" Delphia said. When the two looked at her, she reddened. "My brother Gavin was fond of the songstresses in the taverns lining the Thames. Before he sailed away."

"Ah. Those golden-throated lasses who do warble of the sea. I am surprised John Rowden has a true wife," Jim said. "Most sailors don't."

"He did come home," Art said thoughtfully.

Delphia and Jim knocked on doors to enquire if Mrs Rowden had been seen that night while Art raced away in ghost form to fetch the police. As she flew, she heard a girl scream ahead of her in the fog and paused, thinking her spectral appearance might be the cause. When she found the screamer, the girl did not stare at her but at a man's big feet, sticking stiffly from a church's snow-laden hedge. Art swept aside the snow to reveal him. A policeman lay, his body broken in half. His eyes, though cracked, retained their look of horror.

After seeing to the upset girl, Art raced back for Jim and Delphia.

～

"Mrs Rowden took shelter with a neighbour very late last night, and she was less than coherent and rather distraught," Jim said from the crook of Delphia's arm as she rode Art's shoulder. Art ran down fogged streets, expanding a circle-search from the dead policeman that might reveal more iced victims. She dodged pedestrians, carts, and carriages braving the drifts and thick haze. "However, she left very early this morning when the neighbour took rest. But why did she not send for the police?"

"She saw her husband in her house," Art said, "and now may want her chance to speak to him. I would seek the same were he my beloved."

"Before authorities like ourselves should confront him? Yes. Then we must find him before she does," Jim said. "Hells bells! This ice fog! Our morning is more like twilight!"

Art heard distant ship bells. The buildings Art ran by became dirtier and decrepit. Beggars huddled in doorways, and they heard the cries of a costermonger selling hot eel pies.

"We've left the better streets for seedier ones. We are very near the Thames," Jim said. "Delphia may be right about Rowden seeking that pub."

"There, Art and sir." Delphia pointed.

A large, rough dog lay on its side on the cobblestones, its stiff legs out as if it were a standing statue tipped over.

"It might have succumbed to the natural, brutal weather," Jim said as Art approached it. "What a snarl it has! And its hackles raised. Art could you—oh!" The dog's tail snapped off and tinkled to the stones at the touch of Art's stick. "Well, that's Rowden's work, then."

"He must not kill again," Art said grimly.

"I'd like to know how he does this," Jim said. "The manner of his attack."

"I have given thought, Art and sir, that Captain Buckamore wrote of a 'North Wind, Freya, or demon'," Delphia said.

"And Friend Baffin of a 'she'. We seek an ice spirit. One accompanying John Rowden."

"A Jane Frost?" Jim said.

"Indeed, a Jane Frost, sir," Delphia said. "The captain, in writing of a wind, made me think of that which blows and freezes. That is how I take his meaning."

"Then we should expect a breath that kills. I now understand Buckamore's anger. If Sir Baffin had lived, he'd have kidnapped

Father Christmas next," Jim said.

Art looked up. The fog was moving rapidly around them, but she felt no wind strong enough to push the thick clouds and cause them to run. They billowed along in one direction. Delphia wiped the icy dew from her face.

"Pah," Jim said, spitting moisture. "Might as well be standing by the sea. I think this movement may not be natural."

"Thee speaks my mind," Art said.

She bade Delphia hold on and ran after the tumbling fog.

Several people hurried in the opposite direction Art followed, all looking fearfully behind them. A portly driver clutched his whip as he ran in his long-tailed coat. He held his top hat to his head.

"M-my horse! My horse!" he stuttered, and then ran on.

Art pursued the fog to where it moved swiftest, swirling and then funnelling, right down to the open mouth of a man. He stood in a dark pea coat, waistcoat, tie, and trousers, his black hair slick with moisture. An abandoned carriage stood beside him with a horse frozen stiff. In the open doorway of the tenement building next to the carriage, an old woman stared agape up at the vortex of fog.

Delphia leapt off Art's shoulder and stepped to a position beside the carriage with Jim. At the sound of Delphia's quick steps on the cobblestones, John Rowden's mouth shut. Delphia stopped and Art stilled, watching his back. The whirl of fog slowed around his figure, and he turned his head. He looked at Delphia, and Jim opened his teeth to speak. Art waved him to silence.

"Friend," Art hailed in a gentle tone. "John Rowden. Let me speak with thee."

John did not move.

"John Rowden," Art said. "Husband to Genevieve."

John turned fully around. His gaze was stark and distant, and Art was uncertain if he was capable of recognition or acknowledgement. His moustache was dusted with frost.

"Friend John," she said as she slowly approached. "Can thee hear me? Tell us of the ice spirit. The one brought back on the *Terror*."

John's lips parted.

"*Hhhome*," he said in a high, lost tone.

Art saw ice crystals within his misting breath. They twinkled in the hazy light.

The carriage door banged shut. Two ragged little thieves ran from the vehicle.

John turned at the sound and opened his mouth wide, right before Delphia and Jim.

"Delphia!" Art shouted. She grabbed John by the neck.

Delphia turned and threw Jim into the carriage's open window. The blast of tumbling ice fog that left John's mouth hit the carriage as she dove beneath it, rolled out the other side, regained her feet, and then ran up the steps into the open doorway of the tenement. The woman screamed as Delphia bowled into her, the fog close behind. Art heard her kick the door shut just as the doorway frosted white.

John twisted in Art's grasp, but she held fast. He exhaled more, the plume of his white breath arcing around for Art's face. She backtracked in a circle, dragging him with her. The cloud's crystals touched her upraised fist that clenched her stick.

Blinding, white-hot pain shot through her arm and blackened her eyesight. Her hand felt as though it had been turned 360 degrees and twisted off. Art continued to backpedal, not knowing if the cloud still pursued her. She held her searing limb high above her head. Her wrist was white-fire and she sensed nothing beyond it.

My hand, Art thought. Where *is my hand?*

She stumbled and fell knees-first to the stones, bringing John down with her. As her narrowed vision cleared, she felt him reach behind and pry her fingers off his neck.

He rose and walked into the surrounding ice mist. Art swallowed thickly as he disappeared. When she looked at her injured hand, she saw the fist clenching her stick was pure, translucent crystal.

She heard a door forced open and Delphia's nimble steps.

"Art!" Delphia shouted.

"John Rowden is gone," Art called out.

She swallowed again. The sight of her glasslike hand made her ill.

She heard ice loudly burst on one of the carriage's sealed doors, and then Jim cough.

"Fah! Ha-ha! Nearly burned the seat in there!" he said.

"I'm sorry I left you behind, sir!" Delphia said. "But I was relying on your ability to summon internal fire!"

"No need to apologise, Bloom, that was swift thinking! You knew that of us three, you were the most vulnerable to the frost attack *and* that I could defend myself! As Art and Ellie taught you, you ran to fight another day! Good show!"

Art shakily regained her feet just as the two rounded the carriage. She kept her injured hand and stick away from her body and high above the stones. At the sound of approaching wheels, she walked stiffly to the side of the street. She had no desire to bump into anything.

"Art!" Jim said in a hushed voice when they joined her. "Can you regenerate it?"

"I am willing it," Art said painfully. "'Tis . . . slow."

"Let's find you a safe spot to stand," he encouraged. "Your sturdy back to a wall. Delphia and I will fetch you the sea creatures you need, and once you've ingested, your hand will be as good as resurrected, you'll see!"

Art nodded. "Hurry, Friend."

Art found a tenement wall to stand against and steady her crystallised hand. A few pedestrians on the walk hurried by, startled by her spectral appearance. She was glad of that and that no curious ragged boys emerged from the fog to accost her. As Delphia and Jim ran off into the mist, she cast off wild thoughts of her hand melting.

Her throbbing arm ceased hurting, and that made Art more fearful. She could not bear to look at it. Her poor fist was an ice sculpture fit for a table centrepiece, like the sparkling, weeping ones she'd seen at a Royal Aquarium fête. Yet, John Rowden had managed to harm only her one hand, and Art chastised herself for being so horrified at the occurrence that she had allowed him to escape. She was a regenerating creature, after all, and could possibly grow another if the injured hand broke off. Dr Fall might even give her a mechanical one if that failed.

I am a poor excuse for an agent! Were it Helene injured, she wouldn't dare cry! Art thought. She had yet to shed a tear but felt nearly inclined to do so. *Or . . . Helene might cry. She and Helia are unpredictable.*

A drunkard stumbled down the walk, and his shoulder hit the wall with a resounding *thump*. Art put out her good hand to ward him off and he shambled on, oblivious to her presence.

She inhaled deeply and concentrated on making her fist whole.

By the time Jim and Delphia returned with a basketful of fresh herring from a fishmonger, Art's hand was radiating white-hot pain again. She was encouraged by the searing sensation. It was a signal that by will alone, she had managed to bring some of her flesh back to life. She opened her good hand for the herring, and the fish flew into her body. In that moment of turning translucent to accept the fish, she hoped her solid hand would not fall off. Her body glowed as she digested; the searing pain grew to a blinding sensation, and she cried out.

"*Gah*, Art!" Jim yelled. "I hope that's a good sound!"

Art ceased glowing and held her trembling arm up. Her hand and glove had lost their look of crystal and appeared sound. She opened her burning fingers and saw no icy remnants within, though each awakened digit shot sharp pain through her arm. She slowly let go of her walking stick.

Jim and Delphia both sighed in relief.

"Friends." Art took a deep breath. "Truly, the seamen did not die an easy death."

~

Art needed to exercise the hand even as they moved quickly down the street in which John Rowden had disappeared. Art and Delphia played a game where Delphia tossed Art's stick to her and she caught it, working through the pain her grip caused. The fog was thinning, and more people and vehicles appeared in the wet and sludge of the street. The three came upon the businesses of the Thames: warehouses, tanners, dust yards, potters, brothels, food sellers, and pubs. Yet many, except for the brothels, seemed in a state of inactivity. Warehousemen dawdled by empty wagons, tanners scowled and stood idle, and women in shawls and carrying empty baskets grouped and clucked loudly. Costermongers hurried by with barrows bearing few fish, if any. Art was thinking of buying more to ingest when Jim spoke.

"So! Rowden is the ice-breathing demon."

"With Jane Frost harboured within him," Delphia said. She tossed Art her stick again. "But is he still . . . alive, within his body?"

"Aye, or a reanimation? He did return to his home," Art said in thought. She gave her injury a rest and passed her stick gently from hand to hand. "And the fairy in him spoke the word *home*. Friend Baffin's journal mentioned this as well."

"Indeed!" Jim said. "Hm, indeed! But the possessed Rowden did not sail the *Terror* back to the Arctic. He returned it to his own home, London. Rowden and the fairy's thoughts were the same, only the outcome different. I would say, Delphia, that since he acted on his own desires whilst possessed, that means he's not truly dead."

Art stopped, and Delphia did too. A woman had been following closely behind them, dressed respectably though she wore no hat on her tousled auburn hair and her fine, long coat was opened and concealed an object she held close to her body. She stared at them with wide, lost eyes. Art wondered how much the woman had overheard.

"Can we help you, miss?" Jim said.

She walked quickly past them. The item within her coat flashed, revealing brass. They watched her run swiftly into a crowd of people in the street.

"I—I think she was carrying a blow lamp," Jim said.

Art started. She turned invisible and took off in pursuit. But as she ghosted through the crowd of workmen, costerwomen, and ragged boys, she saw no singular woman of class amongst them. She then flew above, as high up as the thinning fog allowed. Spotting no young woman with auburn hair in the surrounding area and nearby alleyways, she returned to Delphia and Jim, who also searched the crowd.

"Let me guess—no hat on so respectable a woman, and one hat found at the Rowden residence?" Jim said as she materialised before them. "That woman was therefore—"

"Aye, 'twas Genevieve Rowden. She has evaded us."

"She's a fast one," Jim said.

"She must know these surroundings," Art said. "Though she is a respectable woman. Delphia has a gift for this manner of disappearing."

"Well," Delphia said, "when I'm hiding from Hettie O'Taggart."

"This crowd is confounding me," Jim said. "There's a reason for these many disgruntled and congregating. You there, sailor! You look more pleased than the rest. What is happening here?"

"There's a Frost Fair, sir!" the young seaman said excitedly. He looked barely older than Delphia, and from the smell of his breath had already enjoyed gin at the nearest pub. He pointed towards the Thames. "The first in many years! Tents are already put up, and a whole ox is being roasted! A whole ox, sir! The Thames is frozen over and we're 'aving a fair!"

"By golly!" Jim exclaimed as the seaman hurried on. "No wonder the denizens of the Thames are displeased; their livelihoods are at a literal standstill! No boats to unload, no water to dump one's manufacturing offal into. Though we're searching for two quarries now, friends, let's look upon this miracle! I've a thought to share!"

They had only to follow the crowds past the buildings for the quay. Art, being tallest, could spy old signal flags waving from makeshift tents erected upon the River Thames. But the astonishing thing was the river itself.

The Thames was solid, clear ice, and in many places blue, with dirty drifts and tracks of snow. The glassy expanse seemed to stretch from London Bridge to their left all the way past Queen Street Bridge to the right. Art thought the clear ice thick enough that an elephant might walk across it and looked for posted signs warning of thinner or broken ice. She saw none.

She heard sounds of far-off gaiety and saw tiny figures running, falling, and sliding near the fair's tents. A horse walked the solid surface, taking people on sledge rides.

"Thy thought, Friend," Art said.

"Our newly frozen Thames," Jim said. "Right now, its glacial waters are perhaps the coldest spot one could find in London, and with the ice fog thinning, I believe our fairy will seek more cold. Do you know what I noticed in the Rowden parlour?"

Art thought back to the parlour and realised she'd not taken its actual contents into account, having been more concerned with finding the wife.

"A collection of precious cabinet cards," Jim said. "The sort with giant crescent moons as backdrops for the loving Rowden couple to pose before. All taken at various fairs."

They looked out to the tents on the Thames again, the flags waving merrily.

"Let us follow John Rowden to his next memory," Jim said.

Chapter four

There was a slipway down to the ice, and a few yards away from it, a ladder erected, both manned by watermen demanding admittance fare before allowing people down.

"Threepence," the grizzled waterman stated when Art stood at the edge to look below.

"That is no fair price for the waters, for thee does not own them. 'Tis free for all," Art said.

"We own the fair, Quaker. And fer makin' trouble, that'll be six pence, albino!"

"You do not own the fair," Jim said. "And we've great respect for our albino friends. Unlike toothless hags like yourself, which you most certainly resemble, sir. Are you certain you're not Baba Yaga?"

The waterman looked down at him, uncomprehending. Art took Jim from Delphia's hands and knelt.

"Delphia, to my back," she said.

Delphia jumped on to her back and wrapped arms around Art's neck and legs around her waist.

"When thee is ready, say *ready*." Art walked back down the quay. She hefted Delphia so that she might settle more securely.

"Ready!" Delphia said.

Art ran to the quay's edge and leapt. She jumped far enough

to land them with a dull *boom* on the Thames' ice, halfway to the festivities.

Jim crowed, and Art ran them to the fair.

❧

John Rowden emerged from the ice-cooled room of a meat-packing warehouse and stepped out on to the street. Behind him, amongst the shipped refrigeration machines storing Australian beef, men stood frozen. Each time he found perfect cold, he wasted such nourishment on those who disturbed him. He looked up and saw the ice fog thinning in the air. John walked on, looking for more.

The surrounding land of artificial edifices was not like the ice land he had been taken from. He could not know if it would remain cold. But there, on the waters upon which he'd arrived, lay the most intense cold he'd sensed since wandering. He walked to the quay and slowly moved through the crowd to where he could view the thick ice the night had brought, nearly as blue as Arctic glaciers. Beneath that ice was the gelid cold he sought. Then he saw the little tents on the ice and heard the faint strains of music.

That clustering of gaiety was not home, he thought, yet it spoke like it.

People jostled him. There were many gathered around, getting in his way. Too many, more than he could freeze at once. He decided he would act like one of them, join them as they went below. In that way, he would reach the place with the gay flags. The sight of the tents gave him giddy feelings, and he wanted more than just to be near them.

"*The st'nding toast,*" he sang softly. "*That pleas'd the mossst . . .*"

A waterman grabbed him before he could step down the ladder.

"Hold, you! That's threepence!" he said.

John stared, thinking to breathe upon him. Instead, he stepped for the ladder again. The waterman pulled him away once more.

"What are yer, a half-wit? Give us threepence or away with you!"

"*I'm,*" John said in a high, lost voice, "tired *of youuu lot. So tired . . . .*"

"Are you wantin' a knockdown, are yer?" the waterman exclaimed. He shoved John back.

John turned and left. He followed the quay. Below on the ice were more like the waterman, loitering and watching for climbers. John looked for where he could jump down and not waste precious, frigid breath.

～

Art ran to the Frost Fair. Before them were makeshift tents of sails and propped-up oars lined in two rows that stretched from the north bank to the south, creating a lane between them. Smoke rose from some, and the wind drove the scent of roasted meat to their noses.

"Oh, what a smell!" Delphia said.

"I will search the fair for John and Genevieve Rowden. Thee should feed Delphia," Art said.

"This Friend speaks my mind!" Jim jovially agreed.

She dropped them both off in the bustling lane of fairgoers, right by the tent where a vendor roasted mutton, and turned herself invisible. She flew up and down the rows. The enterprising denizens of the Thames' banks were still dragging carts and sledges piled with cheap baubles to the fair proper. More sledges carried bags of coal. Men helped erect a photographer's tent, his giant crescent moon prop of sturdy, painted wood resting nearby, ready to be placed within. The photographer rolled out the painted background he wanted stood up behind the moon.

Art hovered, spotting neither John nor Genevieve Rowden,

and made note to visit the tent again. She flew on and mar-
velled at what had been transported onto the ice in such a short
time; printer's presses, three at her latest count, were churning
out handbills containing commemorative poems or ballads,
and cards personalised with fairgoers' names. Large painted
mechanical children's swings creaked and squeaked, ridden by
adults and children alike. Within a fenced circle off the rows
proper, a butcher had laid sheet metal and a hearth of bricks
to build a great fire. Before it roasted a whole ox skewered on a
thick spit with a weighted wheel on one end, all set on sturdy
trestles with large drip pans beneath. The butcher's assistants
slowly turned and basted the heavy beast while fairgoers paid
sixpence to enter the fence and view the roasting. Outside the
fence, the mounted sign read:

ROASTING OX AT FROST FAIR UPON THE
THAMES SINCE 1788

Art materialised, gave the startled man guarding the fence
sixpence, then ghosted into invisibility again. She floated past
the viewing perimeter and studied the cooking animal up
close, thinking it would need more than a day's roasting to be
done. She judged its weight at over 100 stone. She lingered a
little more to enjoy the pleasurable heat from the great fire, a
sensation that had been absent since her visit to the *Terror* and
especially the freezing of her hand.

Art left the roasting ox and flew past the booths and tents of
a puppeteer, tattooist, fortune-teller, and a gambling den filled
with cigarette smoke. She saw sellers of tea, hot chocolate, coffee, pies, and gingerbread. Temporary pubs with names like
City of Moscow and Country of Lapland sold Old Tom gin,
Mum beer, and a hot, potent, mixture of gin and wormwood
wine called Purl. She saw Helia standing by one pub, Land of
the Arctic, scribbling in her notebook. Her scarf hung loose
and she muttered, her face disquiet. She looked up in wild-eyed
distraction and smiled at the air as Art swept past. Art flew on to

rejoin her partners.

Delphia was ingesting coffee, a minced pie, and a slice of roasted mutton where Art had left them last. Women walked the lane with laden baskets on their heads, selling hot apples. Jim sat on a cider barrel, smoking the last bit of a cheroot. Art materialised next to him and then noticed the manner in which the mutton seller was roasting the shanks of meat. Unlike the butcher in his apron and rolled sleeves, the well-groomed vendor was sharply dressed in full coat, waistcoat, watch chain, and top hat and extolling the virtues of his gas cooking appliance to onlookers. While his assistants carved off slices of cooked mutton for a shilling apiece, he demonstrated how he roasted the spitted meat with a duo of pure-white flames emitted from a standing gas stove. The man tapped at one of the two brass generators beneath with his cane.

"It is the marvel of our modern age!" he exclaimed. "The cleanest of fuels, the simplest to produce, costing you nearly nothing, and with an illuminant as bright and pure as a diamond's!"

"Lady Helene says we ought to keep a safe distance from his acetylene generator, should it leak gas," Delphia said in aside to Art. She polished off her coffee and set the mug down by Jim. "She agrees that acetylene gas is all that he says, but if it should, while oxygenated, escape and meet a flame, it will combust." Delphia looked pointedly at Jim smoking.

"Helene was here?" Art said as she picked up Jim and led Delphia away.

"Art!" Jim said. He gulped his cheroot. "Yes, Lady Helene was just here. I've told her how we've tracked both Mr and Mrs Rowden. She is on the hunt as well."

"Aye, I've spotted her sister and would like to—"

"Oh?" Jim interrupted. "Resume your skirts-chasing? With Delphia replenished and I having smoked a cheroot, we'll now make our own searching round of the fair proper. Did you note anything singular?"

She told him of the photographer's tent. Delphia finished her pie and held her hands out for Jim.

"Thee should walk the rows, and I will fly over the ice fields surrounding the fair," Art said. "After I've spoken to Helia."

"Have a respite, Art!" Jim said. "We certainly did!"

They parted, and Art ghosted, flying back to the pub, Land of the Arctic.

∼

Jim's observation that Helia seemed less a madwoman with each passing day was correct, but Art wondered if ever such a condition could be fully cured. John Rowden harboured an ice fairy, but Helia harboured something darker: an eldritch infection. Sometimes Art could sense its presence when Helia's bewitched mask failed to keep it slumbering. Sometimes when it woke, it drove Helia mad.

"No, no-no-no! Quiet!" Helia hissed to no one in particular as Art flew close. She gripped her notebook and shook her fists at nothing. "We don't drink anymore!"

"Helia," Art said when she alighted. She picked up the ends of Helia's scarf and draped it more securely around her neck.

"Oh! Art!" Helia's gaze focused and her fury vanished. She looked up and brightened, her smile delighted. "Have you finished flying all about the fair?"

"Thee has such a keen sense of me, e'en when I am invisible," Art said.

"I'd know you if you flew all the way to heaven," Helia said, and her smile grew tremulous.

Art bent and kissed her lips. Helia was taller right then; Art noticed she wore ice blades strapped to her boots. She ran her thumb along the leather of Helia's half-mask and could not see nor feel the darkness hiding there. She hoped it would stay asleep, as it usually did, in her presence.

"Thee has been to the Rowden parlour and saw their cabinet cards," Art said, her tone almost accusatory. "Thee has concluded the same, that John Rowden would desire to come here."

"You are correct, dearest," Helia said, her eyes twinkling. "Have you caught the man already?"

"Nearly, but he escaped. His ice breath—"

"Oh? Is that how he does it?"

"Aye. A potent breath it is, for the ice spirit makes use of his body and from it, issues powerful winds." Art considered her words for a moment. "From the mouth, Helia, not from the other end." She raised her right hand. "Such exhalation rendered my fist into glass! 'Twas a frightful injury."

"Oh, Art!" Helia exclaimed and held the fist in both her hands. She kissed it.

After Helia was reassured that all of Art's fingers were in working order, they returned their attention to the matter at hand.

"Genevieve Rowden is also present, somewhere," Art said, "and eludes us. She wants her husband."

"That is understandable. I'd a long discussion with her yesterday; theirs is a strong love. She should have her chance to speak with him."

Art considered it. "'Twill be difficult. But I agree. Will thee skate along with me?" She offered her arm. Helia accepted, and Art strolled while Helia slid along, their arms linked. They departed the row and stepped into the Thames' greater ice fields where more people skated, sledged, and bowled at ninepins. Helia pointed to a woman standing farther out on the ice, working at a painter's folding easel.

"Miss Wila Stanchfield, the other woman illustrator for the *Strand*. Aldosia can't be bothered with illustrating frivolity, no matter how singular the event. She deems such gaieties worthy of only *Punch* caricaturists and cartoonists." Helia leaned into Art, her tone low. "I'm afraid she and Wila are not very fond of each other."

She then looked at Art expectantly. "Is this sufficient distance from the fair, dear?"

Art smiled. "Before Jim and I arrived at the *Terror*, Helene could have taken the queer metal hidden in Friend Baffin's bedding," she said.

Helia grinned ruefully and her gaze dropped. "True," she said. "But she didn't."

"Then thee are interested in those strange pieces. 'Tis fortunate thee are not evil," Art said gently.

Helia looked up at her, her gaze stark.

"I hope we're not," she whispered.

"I can tell thee what we suspect of the ice spirit," Art said. "That which resides in John Rowden."

Helia's face brightened again. She looked at Art expectantly.

"We think 'tis Jane Frost," Art whispered.

Helia covered her mouth in mirth.

"'Tisn't so strange a thought!" Art protested.

Helia hugged her arm.

"I'll tell you what we suspect of the metal," she whispered. "We think it may not be of Earth."

Art looked at her, uncertain what to make of the information.

"Not of Earth . . . like Jim and I?"

Helia laughed. "No, dearest. I don't mean supernatural or from the Fourth Dimension. I mean, quite literally: it is not of Earth."

She pointed up into the sky. Art looked up once, then twice.

"Thee means . . . from the *moon*?" Art whispered in astonishment. "Or Saturn, or—another heavenly sphere? Have I the substance of what thee is saying, Helia?"

"Yes, Art, we are talking about what's beyond there. Of a world perhaps very far away," Helia softly said. "Made all of ice."

Art stared, wide-eyed, trying to imagine it. "Yet how?" she finally asked. "What vessel could come from such a place to here?"

Helia held Art's hand to the rosy cheek not covered by her half-mask. Art brushed the softness.

"What vessel, indeed," Helia whispered.

～

While watching the games and antics, Art thought to resume her search for John Rowden on the ice field itself, but Helia stayed her.

"Helene is already doing that, Art."

"But Helia, I can do so faster," Art protested. "'Tis nothing that can move as fast as when I'm—"

A three-wheeled land yacht suddenly swept by them, the tall, single sail catching wind. Helene sat within the wagon and worked the levers, a dashing figure in black with her tricorne, long coat, and grey scarf flying behind her. She glanced at them as she sped along, and Art saw that she wore blue-tinted lenses clipped over her spectacles. Soon she was but a tiny figure in the distance, smoothly turning the sail and arcing the yacht around the fair's end. She and the craft disappeared beyond the tents. Well-dressed young bucks at that end of the ice whooped and waved their hats after her.

"Sky-court! Sky-court!" they faintly cheered.

"Well," Art said. "As she has such a pretty craft . . . she may make search of the ice, then."

"The yacht belongs to those young men, Art. Helene is only borrowing it," Helia said. "They kept pitching the poor thing into drifts. Oh! It makes me miss feluccas."

"Which thee pitched into . . . ?"

"The River Nile." Helia giggled.

"Helene is well-accepted amongst boys," Art said.

"Yes, she is. She's even been offered memberships into their gentlemen's clubs, like the Explorers' Club." Helia sniffed. "Only a male impersonator has ever managed that."

"'Tis why she has Vesta membership," Art exclaimed in re-alisation. "'Twas given to her by Catherine Moore. I thought it a queer choice for Helene. A club with tigers and swords and bomb-ships would suit her better," she added under her breath.

"When you've a family that owns airships, Art, people hardly refrain from bestowing privilege. I suspect it's why our society tolerates my asylum stays and scandalous desire for a profession."

"Thee likes to work. And Helene lives the ascetic's life and eschews most privileges. Thee are both remarkable women despite being born into class."

Helia hugged her arm as Helene sailed by again. They watched her reach the far end of the fair and slow the yacht to a stop by the cheering bucks. Helene disembarked and looked in their direction.

"So many circles with the yacht, and no John Rowden, else she would have stopped to tell us so," Helia said.

"Oh? And not handle the ice fairy herself?"

"She's no longer the Blackheart, Art," Helia whispered.

"She still remains that masked heroine of the night, Helia," Art said gently. "Slayer of creatures. No more able to stay idle than I could, were I somehow retired from the Secret Commission."

Helia hugged Art's arm to her. Art squeezed her hand.

"Let us visit the gingerbread seller," Art suddenly said. "Then I'll be ready to greet thy sister."

Helene laughed as she pulled her back to the fair's rows.

∽

Genevieve Rowden peeped warily from the back flaps of a tent where chowder was served and watched Miss Skycourt and the Secret Commission agent leave the ice for the fair proper. She'd taken a great chance coming to the fair, with the hope that somehow John would find himself there. She felt he would, despite the creature inside him. As the agents had said, he had come home after all. If he were still her John, he would want to visit a place so similar to the fair where they first met.

She yearned to speak to the journalist again. She was exhausted, at times filled with dread or fear for John, and desperately wished for a sympathetic ear or counsel. But right then she dared not, especially when Miss Skycourt was clearly an acquaintance of the agents. Resigned, she withdrew within the tent. She'd given the proprietor a shilling to shelter her, and he was more than happy to oblige. While she waited for John to appear, she busied herself with helping the wife lay out the soup bowls needing ladling.

~

Art purchased three pieces of warm gingerbread and had each wrapped in paper. One she gave to Helia, the second went into her coat pocket, and the third she also pocketed for Delphia.

But she still needed to fly the ice and look for John Rowden. Her forsaken promise to make that search nagged at her. Helia had agreed to meet her where fairgoers skated once she was done. Art turned invisible and sped around the ice surrounding the fair, spying the wheel tracks Helene had made with the land yacht. She flew farther and looked at the people who came down ladders, sideways, or trooped in anticipation across the ice. She peeked at the painting on which Miss Stanchfield worked, thought it lovely, and then flew around Helene, who walked slowly and determinedly across the ice towards the fair. In the distance, the young bucks sailed their land yacht. They promptly caught the wrong wind and tipped. Art saw Delphia and Jim speed along on purchased blades, following the fair's outer perimeter. Delphia's strides were strong and smooth, and Art wondered how much skating Delphia had indulged in before her family's fall from the middle class. Art entered a tent at

the fair's end and flew through each successful stall. She ghosted through cooks, sellers, goods, stoves, pots, barrels, coal sacks,
gamblers, performers, printing presses, engravers, and drinking
patrons. But when she entered the fortune-teller's dark tent, the
woman screamed, her gaze seemingly on her invisible form.

"Ghost! *Ghost!*" she shrieked. "Ghost flying!"

～

Genevieve nearly dropped a bowl of chowder at the screams
of the medium in the tent next door. She ran out the back flaps,
bowl still in hand. She dared not look behind her should the
ghost-agent somehow spy her face.

～

Chagrined, Art swiftly passed from the distraught fortune-
teller's presence into a stall serving steaming chowder, and seeing neither John nor Genevieve Rowden, ghosted on.

Art finally returned to where Helia stood, behind a tent row,
her back to the skaters and ice field. Art materialised and wondered what Helia was looking at within the fair's lane. Noticing
her, Helia smiled and pointed; just within their line of sight
and in the row across stood the photographer's tent, the man
busy behind his camera as four sailors posed with the crescent
moon. Delphia skated to Art and Helia and came to a stop,
then bent over to catch her breath.

"Miss Skycourt has the same idea, I see!" Jim said. "And look
there! Lady Helene has reached this spot as well."

Art looked back to the ice. Many who played on it lacked
blades and made do by slipping and sliding along, gathering
snow to throw or playing in drifts, building snowmen. But
among such revellers, Helene stood erect and still. Her eyes
were closed behind her tinted spectacles, her palms pressed
together as if in prayer, and one raised leg pointed a bent knee
to the side. Art thought she might rest the foot of that bent knee

against her standing leg, for she saw that beneath Helene's skirts she stood on one foot.

"Silly goose!" Helia said, looking towards Helene. "She stands in *vrksasana*—like a tree."

"With one boot sole upon the bare ice?" Art exclaimed. "'Tis a feat, this yogi!"

"*Yoga*, dear Art," Helia corrected with a brief smile. She returned her attention to Helene and sniffed. "I don't know why she's engaging in meditation right this minute."

"Delphia!" Jim said. "You could practice some of your yogah!"

"Certainly, sir," Delphia said. "When I'm not wearing blades, and falling down upon them. We now know I remember how to skate forwards, but backwards is something I never learned."

"Delphia, I'll show you how one skates backwards," Helia said. She stepped backwards on to the ice, her arms out as she smiled invitingly to Art, then kicked off with a foot. She smoothly slid, each of her backward steps curving then kicking out, propelling her around the ice. Just like when riding her penny-farthing, Helia hardly bothered to look about her, yet somehow avoided collisions—though more accurately, people avoided colliding with her.

"Art," Jim said, "I'll keep watch on the photographer and for Mr and Mrs Rowden. Delphia, you study Miss Skycourt's technique. Now, Art, go!"

Art ghosted and swept across the ice, following the paths Helia carved backwards. Helia made her way to Helene and cut circles around her while Art flew around and around in her wake. She touched Helia's outspread hands and felt her glide, her gaze on Helia's twinkling eyes. Helia winked. She continued to cut across the ice backwards, and Art sailed. Finally, Helia skidded to a stop near Delphia. Art alighted and solidified beside her.

Helene abandoned her stance, looked towards the three, and

slowly advanced. A boy fell and slid by her. A man lost his footing and began desperately running in place until he too fell and slid painfully away, his sweetheart exclaiming and then laughing. Helene's stride remained firm. Not once did her soles slip.

"Cheat!" Helia accused when Helene came before them. Art looked at them both in surprise.

"Now, now," Helene said to Helia. She then glanced up at Art as if to speak. Art took that moment to pat her coat pocket.

Helene gazed over her spectacles, incredulous. Art patted her pocket again.

"'Tisn't a mousetrap," she said.

"It's a most wonderful thing! Oh, Helene, go on!" Helia said. "Then I can eat mine!"

At Helia's words, Helene plunged her gloved hand into Art's pocket and pulled out the paper-wrapped package.

"And one for Delphia," Art said, pulling out the other wrapping. She held it out.

"Oh, thank you, Art!" Delphia said.

When Art turned back to Helene, she had her paper open and was staring at the warm gingerbread.

"I can carry the treat for thee," Art suggested. "'Tis unseemly for a respectable woman to eat before the—"

Helene proceeded to take a large bite out of her gingerbread while Helia bit hers with dainty enthusiasm. Seeing the ladies eat their treats, Delphia followed suit.

"Ha-ha!" Jim said. "Tea and biscuits!"

"I shall find a hot-chocolate seller," Art said, smiling.

～

They were making merry, Art knew, with John Rowden still roaming and possibly freezing people right then. They were supposed to be watching the photographer's tent. But she wanted the precious moment. For work like theirs, the soul and body needed their time of renewal, and Art was delighted to watch the twins and Delphia enjoy their gingerbread and hot chocolate. Jim, resting in Art's hand, partook of a cigarette and swivelled about, watching the activity around them.

"Thee is taller today," Art observed as Helene drank the hot chocolate she'd purchased for her. "Thee is now thy sister's height."

"Well, if you must know," Helene said. She raised a boot, exposing the sole. Strapped to the bottom was a metal plate with the long tips of metal screws pointed outward.

"How deadly!" Art exclaimed.

"They are ice claws," Helene said.

"Cheat," Helia muttered.

Jim gulped his cigarette. "There's our man," he said.

They all turned to the ice field. In the distance a small ice cloud tumbled along the surface and came rapidly towards the fair. Within it stood a man in a pea coat, dusted white: John Rowden.

CHAPTER FIVE

John meandered down the quay long enough to pass Queen Street Bridge and lose sight of the fair. More discontented watermen guarded sideways and ladders, demanding fare of people wanting to explore the ice or bring down objects to sledge in. On the ice were a few ill-looking tents and sparse attempts at creating fair enclaves. But John didn't like the look of them.

He tried to discard desire for the gay place with flags and seek broken ice. The entity inside wanted the nourishment of ice waters, but it also did not like that they'd strayed farther from the ship in which they'd arrived. The *Terror* lay in the other direction, beyond the gay fair and London Bridge. The more John walked, the less likely it seemed that the river's ice would break up; he had to go back. But first, he was weary of being apart from perfect cold. He moved for the side of the quay and climbed down. Watermen below hurried to his location and shouted when he dropped to the ice. He turned and faced them.

"You!" they yelled. "Pay yer fare!"

John pursed his lips and blew.

His white breath struck the first man in his upraised arm, another in his face, and the third in his hand. The men screamed, and the one whose face was frozen clawed at it, breaking away shards of iced flesh. They flailed and fell. John watched as the man with the frozen arm snapped his limb off at the place of impact.

John turned away, satisfied. He had finally learned that, as with the ghost woman, just a little ice could stop people. He walked on through dirty drifts and stepped onto the ice. It was sturdy and thick like the home from which he had been taken. How long could he survive when it finally went away, like the snow around him?

For the snow of the place, its chill was weak. It became slush and melted. It stank of chemicals. The entity within John could not sleep in such snow and wait for the river to reveal itself again. It needed to escape very soon, and it needed the water.

But first, the fair. He'd return to it. He drew on the ice beneath his feet, and a white, freezing cloud built around him. The ice thinned as he sucked fog into his mouth and his feet began to glide, surrounded by the whirling shards he pulled from the frozen surface. The force propelled him along. He glided all about in paths of figure eights and circles, turning white from the swirling crystals.

John rode his cloud back to Queen Street Bridge and under it. He saw the fair in the distance and slid swiftly for it.

At the sight of John Rowden, revellers on the ice stopped and gaped. Miss Stanchfield peered around her easel. Jim shouted from Art's hand.

"Let him in!" he cried. "Let him enter the fair! But we *must* move all the people away from him!"

"Jim?" Art said in surprise. "Such a chance thee takes, but I will follow thy leading!"

She reached up, grabbed a tent's canvas, and ripped it down, startling the occupants. She urged them away. John Rowden's

cloud slowed at the perimeter of the tents. Art wanted him
to have plenty of room to come within the lane and not feel
impelled to release his deadly breath. Delphia pulled out her
blackthorn cudgel from within her coat and brandished it, urg-
ing startled fairgoers back.

"Move away!" Delphia ordered loudly. "Move away, all of
you! Unless you want to be as dead as the men of the *Terror!*"

Helene brought her hands up and by her authoritative presence, forced people to press back.

"Move back or *die* like the men of the *Terror!*" she shouted.

"Oh! Aldosia should not have missed this," Helia said by Art's
side. She entered the lane and scrambled away on her blades.
Art nearly wanted to follow, but John Rowden passed right then
before her, his gaze wide as he looked up at the flapping flags.
He stepped into the Frost Fair's lane.

"Art! A word," Jim yelled up to her.

Art brought him to her ear, tucked her stick beneath one
arm, and grabbed protesting people with the other. She lifted
them out of the way and used her body to move more people
back while Delphia ran ahead and cleared a path for John. All
the while Art kept abreast of him as he slowly walked down the
lane, his ice smoke puffing about his legs. He turned his head
this way and that, seemingly taking in his surroundings.

"Art, I want to try something," Jim said urgently. "I know it
goes against our usual modus operandi, but for now, let's not
confront him. Physically, I mean. We'll keep the fairgoers away,
that's key. But I want my chance to reason with the ice creature."

"Thee remember how our last encounter ended," Art said.

"Yes, but look at him now. No longer breathing on any who
screams, or makes a noise, or a move of similar disruption! I
think he wants to be here, at this fair, more than he wants to ice
us to oblivion. It is a risk, but if we can keep everyone back, only
we would fall victim should he want to defend himself."

"I agree with thy willingness to deal plainly with the creature. 'Tis the manner of Friends. But Helene may not agree."

"Ah, because she was once that one who rode—"

Art placed a hand over his teeth, appalled. "Jim!" she harshly whispered.

She removed her hand and looked for Helene. She was across the lane, arms out to keep the fairgoers back. Her black-clad figure was taut with coiled power while her bright gaze was on John.

"I enjoyed how she brought down the Living Gargoyle!" Jim whispered into Art's ear.

"Jim, hush!"

John stopped. His ice cloud slowly dissipated. The clamour of the fairgoers died down, and all heads turned to see what he looked at.

He'd reached the photographer's tent. Genny stood before it with Helia by her side. Art tossed Jim to Delphia and rushed across the lane to hold Helene back.

"Give her time to—" Art said.

"Give the wife a chance to—" Helene said. She trapped Art's wrist to her own body, as if to hold Art back as well.

"What? Thee is of the same mind?" Art said in surprise.

"Hush, *hush!*" Jim called.

Genny stepped away from Helia and approached John. Her gaze was stark and her steps weary. Art steeled herself and Helene grip her tightly.

"John," Genny said. "Are you in there?"

John stared and softly exhaled. A puff of ice fog left his lips, filled with tiny, winking crystals.

"Speak to me, John," she demanded. "I want John to speak to me!"

They watched each other, John motionless and silent as if trying to comprehend Genny's words. His lips parted.

"*The lasss that loved a sssailorrr,*" he softly sang.

Genny pressed her hand to her mouth.

John looked past her and to the photographer's tent with its crescent moon prop.

"*Moooon . . .,*" John whispered.

Genny dropped her hand.

"*You* come out of my John," she said.

She brought up a large brass paraffin blow lamp. She pumped it, smoke curling from the burner head. It ignited with a bright flash, and a two-foot long blue flame roared from the head. She pointed the flame at John's feet.

John's mouth opened wide and emitted a piercing scream. Though the flame did not touch his shoes, the ice rapidly turned to liquid near them.

"Burn, then!" Genny shouted above the flame's roar. "Burn, or come out! John could live with one foot!"

A blue, gelatinous cloud tumbled from John's mouth, twinkling with suspended ice flints. The flashing particles rained up and coalesced above Genny's head, the shape almost female. It pulled the tail of its smoke from John's mouth, and he crumpled to the ice.

Mermaid? Art thought.

"Djinn?" Jim exclaimed.

Art stared at the sparkling, blue creature filled with tiny, winking crystals and wondered why she thought of the sea.

Genny stepped back.

"Don't you *dare* freeze me!" she cried.

"Genevieve, no!" Helia shouted.

Art and Helene let go of each other and moved.

Genny lifted the blow lamp and pointed the blue flame at the creature. The cloud flew for her face and she screamed.

It rushed into her mouth and disappeared. Genny dropped the roaring lamp, and it bounced on the ice.

Both Helene and Art grabbed for her. But it was Helene who snatched Genny out from under Art's grasp and dragged her quickly to an open cider barrel. She plunged Genny's head into it and held her down. Genny's arms slapped the barrel frantically, and the cider sloshed.

"Helene! What are you doing?" Art cried.

"What does it look like I'm doing? I'm drowning her!" Helene said.

"Kill not the woman if thee wants to kill the ice spirit!" Art said and grabbed Helene as Genny's arms faltered, then went slack. Art dragged Helene back while Delphia pulled Genny's soaked head out. Helene struggled in Art's grip.

"Art! I'm not trying to kill her, I'm just trying to—"

Genny threw her head back and exhaled, expelling the blue cloud that twinkled with shards like diamonds. Helia leapt forwards in Art's arms. The cloud rushed into Helene's mouth and disappeared.

Helene shook and her body chilled in Art's grip. Her eyes became icy pale.

"Helene!" Art shouted.

Helene rammed the top of her head into Art's chin, and Art's head snapped back.

CHAPTER SIX

Art woke to Helia smacking her cheek.

"How—how long?" she uttered, stumbling to her feet.

"Hardly a minute, Art! Helene has gone down the row! I'm certain she's up to something, but I can't guess what! You must stop her!"

"Is Helene not possessed?" Art said in confusion, recalling how the ice spirit had entered Helene's body.

"She is! It's just—" Helia fixed Art's hat, then pointed down the row. "Oh, Art, go!"

Art ghosted and flew. She passed through the crowd blocking the lane and saw Delphia and Jim. Helene had thrown down the mutton seller's stovetop and driven him and his assistants out. The mutton shanks followed, hitting the lane and causing a surge for the meat just when Art solidified. She stumbled in the sudden crush and nearly ghosted again. Then she saw people fall underfoot. She grabbed them up and shoved the rest back. Helene ripped up a tent pole and collapsed the mutton seller's tent into the next, causing more to topple. Art heard people scream within the wreckage, and she ghosted through the confusion. She pulled people out and stomped on a spreading cooking fire.

Why does the ice spirit do this? she thought. *'Tis more Helene's thinking!*

Then Helene grabbed one of the acetylene generators. Art dropped the people in her hands.

Helene swung the generator far into the ice field, sending it bouncing.

"*Gas!*" Jim bellowed. "*Run,* everyone run!"

Art ghosted as people ran screaming through her. Helene looked towards the ice and snapped her right arm straight out. A single-shot percussion derringer popped from her black sleeve and into her hand. She pulled the folding trigger and fired.

The generator jumped. It exploded in a bright-white flash, and an ear-shattering blast sounded. The air rippled and brass bits embedded everywhere. Women screamed. Chunks of ice rained down, and Art heard a great cracking sound. Floes floated in the newly revealed, frigid water while more ice crumbled down the nearly two-foot-thick sides. Helene had blown a hole in the Thames.

Helene picked up the second generator and spun in a circle on her heel—once, twice, then threw the heavy canister at Art, who solidified and caught it. People screamed more and scrambled away. Art stared aghast as Helene snapped up her arm and the pistol popped from her sleeve again. She pointed the barrel at her.

"Art!" Helia cried, pushing through the fleeing crowd. "Her derringer only fires a single—"

Art heaved and threw the generator up in the air. It flew high and arced far away, disappearing in the low clouds.

"But could she not reload, Helia?" Art exclaimed.

"Art!" Jim yelled. "What will happen when that gas lands?"

Art looked at Helene in frustration. "*Thee!*"

She ghosted and flew swiftly for the sky.

Helene lowered her arm, and the derringer withdrew into her sleeve. She turned for the hole in the Thames and walked towards it.

"Helene!" Helia cried and stomped her foot. "Stop that, stop it right now!"

Delphia jumped the remains of the mutton seller's tent and skated out onto the ice. She swerved to a stop between the hole and Helene. Before she and Jim could act, the land yacht sped towards them. It slowed between the two, and the young men aboard loudly accosted.

"Skycourt!" they yelled. "What are you doing?"

"Men!" Jim cried. "You're confronting a gentlewoman! She's bound to—"

Helene's arm came up, wrist by her face. Her fingers held a bright blade. She whipped her arm down.

"—defend herself!" Jim yelled as Delphia dove for the ground. The flying blade snapped a sail rope in two. The pieces whipped, and the canvas caught one last wind before it tumbled down. The craft skidded across the ice, tilted, and dumped its passengers. The young bucks slid away.

"Oh, bad luck!" Jim said. "They're down. Can't say we'll stop her, but maybe we can delay! I'll be your blow lamp, Bloom! Let's have at her, *hokahey*!"

Delphia skated swiftly towards Helene, just as Helene's foot whipped out before her, arcing in an outside kick. The tips of her ice claw flashed, and Delphia veered. She let Jim go just as he burst into flames and blew fire straight at Helene.

Helene opened her mouth and exhaled pure white fog, engulfing Jim and his fire. The fog turned black. She continued to blow until her billowing cloud of ice slowly became white again. She shut her lips and the fog gently dissipated.

Jim dropped into Helene's hands, encased in a rough cocoon of crystal. The ice before his face was blackened with the smoke he'd ejected.

Helene drew back her arm. She sent him bowling across the ice.

Whack.

Delphia kicked Helene's legs out from under her, bringing her cudgel down on Helene's chest as Helene fell backwards. Helene put a hand down on the ice, flipped over Delphia's cudgel, and regained her footing. With a short kick, she knocked the weapon from Delphia's grip and sent it clattering down the ice.

Delphia wobbled on her blades, then put her fists up.

"That's it, Delphia!" Helia shouted. "Give her your best bulldog! Grr!"

Delphia dropped her fists and skated away.

The fairgoers groaned and yelled. Delphia rounded on her blades and raced back towards Helene. As she gained speed, she turned and kicked up. She leapt, arms spread, and threw her body at Helene.

"Yes! Knock her down!" Helia cried.

Helene grabbed her out of the air and twisted. Delphia's blades hit the ground. They spun. Helene's fist popped into Delphia's chest just as she let her go.

The blow sent Delphia speeding down the ice backwards. She turned her blades to halt her trajectory, and ice flints flew. Once she stopped, she raised her fists again.

"One—moment," Delphia said.

Her legs crumpled and she plopped down on the ice. Dazed, she clutched her chest. The fairgoers cheered and some rushed to help her stand. Before they could push her back into the fray, Helene stepped for the hole again.

Helia skidded to her side and grabbed her arm.

"You difficult—ninny—just vomit the thing!" she cried. "How do you know it won't keep you down there?"

Helene seized the lapels of Helia's coat, and Helia seized Helene's in turn. Helene swung around, attempting to fling her.

Helia's legs flew, but she landed easily, her blades skidding. Not once did she release Helene.

"No you don't! No! No! Monkey!" Helia said as they grappled.

Helene suddenly picked her up by the waist. Helia shrieked.

"Hoorah!" the crowd cheered.

Art flew down.

She dropped a coil of rope near Delphia, who wobbled but stood. Then she landed by the twins and pulled them apart. She held Helene away by the throat and set Helia down. Helene dug fingers hard into the back of her hand, and Art gritted her teeth, ignoring the pain. She handed Helia her stick, removed her hat, and handed that to her as well.

"Art, what are you planning?" Helia gasped.

"Thee be ready to revive thy sister," Art said.

She gave Helia a gentle push and sent her sliding yards away. Art then called to Delphia.

"Have thy looped rope in hand, and when thee sees me changed, catch me tight!"

Helene reached over and grabbed Art's chest muscle nearest the armpit. She clenched it.

Art gave an agonised sound and loosened her grip. Helene shrugged out of her fingers, jumped, and punched her in the face.

Art held her nose and looked at Helene, incredulous. "If thee wishes to enrage me, thee cannot!"

Helene leapt again and kicked up, arcing her leg from the outside and sending her foot high above her head.

"Art! Beware her heel!" Helia cried.

Just as Helene brought her heel down like a hammer, the ice claw raking, Art ghosted. She solidified when Helene landed and took firm hold of Helene's shoulders, driving her knee up.

"Guh," Art uttered as Helene caught her knee and stabbed a sharp elbow into the top of her thigh.

"Oh!" Helia exclaimed. "And beware her nerve strikes!"

Art could not reply because Helene then rammed her elbow into the side of her thigh.

Leg deadened, Art hobbled in agony. She took hold of Helene's attacking arm, slipped on the ice, and fell to her knees, taking Helene down with her. Helene dropped to a knee, swivelled, then punched Art's grabbing arm in the shoulder, near the armpit.

"Agh," Art emitted as her arm died. She lost hold of Helene.

Helene drove a knuckle into the nerves between Art's throat and clavicle.

The fairgoers cheered as Art curled in anguish. Helene rose and turned once more for the broken ice.

"Oh—thee! Would cheer," Art grated, "for the littler one! Possessed though she may be!"

She lunged for the ends of Helene's long coat. With a sharp tug, she forced Helene to land on her behind and dragged Helene against her. She wrapped an arm around her throat like a vise. Art gripped her opposing bicep to lock the hold, then brought her free hand down to press on the back of Helene's head.

"Argh," Art uttered when Helene elbowed her sharply in the injured thigh again.

With a deep breath she tensed her arm. She gently squeezed into the sides of Helene's neck, slowly compressing the carotid arteries. Helene grabbed Art's pressing hand and pulled back on the middle finger, forcing Art to give her the hand. Helene then pulled the finger back even more. Art pressed her head to Helene's in agony.

"No, sweetling, this must be done," she said. "I am sorry."

She tightened her chokehold around Helene's neck and watched Helene's grip on her finger falter. Helene sagged and dropped the hand. When she snored, Art knew Helene was not pretending. She promptly released her and covered her mouth with hers.

To me, she urged the ice spirit.

A churning cold pour into her that sent pounding pain through her face and made her skull numb. The diamond lights rushed to the very tips of her fingers and toes and possessed her meat and bones. She was a vessel of water, of ice breath, and from her eyes another being stared.

Art parted lips with Helene and sucked in the lingering tail of gelatinous, blue smoke.

✂

Art rose and stumbled away while Helia skated swiftly to her sister. She grabbed Helene's legs, lifted them, and watched for signs of revival. Helene abruptly woke with a snort.

"Delphia!" Helia cried.

Delphia streaked across the ice on her blades, twirling a large loop of rope above her head by her wrist. She threw it and lassoed Art around her middle, pinning her arms. Art jerked her arms free, and Delphia snapped back the rope, tightening it at Art's waist. Art limped for the broken ice, dragging Delphia.

Home, Art thought.

Her injured leg collapsed and she fell. She rolled to her belly as her body slid. Like a great spectral seal, she rode on her chest right into the water.

Art hit the glacial waters face-first and all bodily sensation fled. Her head became mere dead weight, dragging her body farther down into the dark. Pure, pressing cold enveloped and pierced her bones. She was stone, sinking, and her limbs lost feeling. The entity within her stretched for the gelid deep.

Thee calls thyself Diamond, Art thought in wonder.

Yesss, the entity whispered.

Why did thee not leave the Terror *and join the sea?* Art thought.

This, not my ocean, the entity answered. *Not cold. Need*

Home's.

In her mind's eye, Art saw a tumultuous ice ocean beneath a blue, glacial land. The black sky above held strange constellations and a great, ringed heavenly sphere.

Thee is of stars, Art thought.

She opened her mouth.

Her breath left and the ice being emerged. In the great black, Art thought she saw twinkling diamonds whirl. But she could not tell if it was what her eyes truly saw or if it was her body's last electrical messages, shown behind her eyelids.

Thump.

The dull blow to the top of her head jarred her awake. Something pulled hard at her waist, and Art burped water. Was she still upside down? Had she hit debris at the bottom? She was aware of none of her limbs, but she sought to raise them. She felt her middle pulled upon again. Her deadened hands brushed along ice above her head, then broke water. Something grabbed them.

Ouch, Art thought as her face scraped ice, though she felt nothing. Her head broke surface and she gurgled, coughing up water. Helene lay chest-down on a ladder at the ice's very edge, pulling on Art's hands. She braced her feet on a rung. She grabbed both of Art's forearms, and Art forced her numb fingers to grasp Helene's in turn. She watched in dismay as her fingers disobeyed.

"I have you," Helene said firmly.

Men and women pulled hard on the rope tied to the ladder, and Delphia and more helpers pulled on Art's rope. Ice crumbled down, but Helene's grip was steadfast. They heaved her out of the Thames and slid her waterlogged body to safe ice. Art vomited up more water in front of Helene.

Helene scrambled to her feet, climbed over Art, and kneed her in the back.

"Blorp," Art wetly ejected, and coughed the last of the

Thames up. Her burning lungs inhaled scant air, and her eyes closed.

"Don't nap now, Art," Helene ordered.

Art heard Helia skid to their side.

"Oh, Art! Ghost!" she cried.

Art forced her eyes open and concentrated. Nothing happened. She lay cheek to the ice and felt no cold. With her body numb, her brain had lost the ability to cause change. As far as she knew, she had no legs. And her breath came slowly; too slowly. She would sleep and suss out how to turn transparent another time.

"I apologise for this, darling," Helene said.

'Darling'? Art thought.

Then Helene trod on the hand Art could see. She watched Helene's ice claws dig in.

Alarmed, Art ghosted. The freezing water within and without fell splashing from her ghost body. She reappeared in solid form, nearly dry but madly shivering.

"Ah," Helene said with satisfaction. "Now you're living."

CHAPTER SEVEN

Evening fell on the frozen Thames. The Frost Fair sellers lit lamps and fires, and rowdy men and women filled the chilled air with boisterous words and laughter. Art sat with her back against coal sacks, blankets beneath her and over her shivering body, right near the great hearth fire roasting the ox. Jim's ice crystal sat closer to the fire and was more than half melted, leaving a puddle beneath. The butcher's people charged fair-goers more pence to view HRH Secret Commission agents thaw. Helia sat under the blankets with her, her body warm. She chortled to herself and typed on a barebones typewriter contraption, held in the hand with a dial to choose letters of the alphabet. After typing several strips of paper that Art assumed was part of her story for the *Times*, she pocketed the device and hugged Art.

Helene, Helia told her, was making recompense to the mutton seller, land yacht owners, and other aggrieved persons harmed by her rampage. She'd also had "Mind the Hole" signs made for the patch of ice she'd damaged. Delphia ran back and forth to the tea seller, bringing Art cups of hot tea, her energy still high and possibly fuelled by more coffee and minced pies. When Jim's jaw finally came free of ice, they inspected him for fragility. He had retained his bony sturdiness despite his freezing, but his teeth chattered so much, Delphia whisked him away to find a stove he could sit on.

Every nerve point on Art's body that had met Helene's elbow or fist still hurt, but she wasn't about to complain. Despite her own chattering teeth, Art tried to ask about the ice spirit. She knew she had rid the fair of its danger, but she also allowed it to escape.

"Dearest, it was the best you could do, especially when faced with Helene," Helia comforted. "And well, Helene said that whilst possessed by the ice fairy, she'd the same plan as you—"

"Did she? 'T-twas no question I should go into the ice, not her!" Art exclaimed. "T-too much chance of her being held below, when she is human a-and more capable of dying."

Helia clasped her shaking hand. "In this, I am in full unity with thee," she said.

Art's heart swelled to hear her speak in the manner of Friends. She gave Helia a quick kiss, and they rested their heads together.

"Helene and I had discussed the fairy before you and Mr Dastard arrived at the fair," Helia said. "I knew she'd come to certain conclusions but wouldn't share. Had she, I would have vehemently disagreed with her plan. We couldn't know how long Helene would keep her own awareness under its influence." Helia paused, then said in a low voice, "And someone like Helene should not be manipulated by anything. We have our airships to consider."

Art remembered how the ice entity had felt when it was inside her. She didn't think it would care to control airships, but it was a legitimate concern.

"You did wonderfully, dear," Helia whispered, smiling. "Think no more of how to pursue the fairy, for truly, the answer is 'nothing'. With Mr Dastard still in thaw and you having survived the frigid Thames—if the creature lies sleeping beneath

us or is swimming, we will discover later. Even Helene thinks
the matter done."

Art shivered and had to be content with that.

Beyond the fire, another couple lay beneath blankets, and
Art was satisfied that at least one aspect of the matter was re-
solved. Genny Rowden lay embracing her pallid husband,
keeping him warm. A few drunken seamen broke through the
crowd of roast-watchers and wandered nearer the fire. Before
the butcher's assistants could force them back, one looked at
Genny, then pointed.

"I know you!" he said in a loud voice. "You're Genny Tilly,
the rose-cheeked girl who warbled at the Swan."

"I don't know what you mean," she said.

"Sing us 'The Lass That Loves a Sailor'."

The butcher's assistants dragged him away, leaving the two
in peace.

"Genny," John hoarsely whispered.

Genny closed her eyes and hugged him tightly.

"We don't know if he'll last the night," Helia whispered to
Art. "Much less the next hours. He had harboured the creature
for too long. Genny has decided to keep him here, amongst
all this cheer. With the smell of roasted meat and the boisterous crowds. It was how they first met, surrounded by revellers."
Helia looked at them, her smile bittersweet. "That night, in seaman's fashion, he fought men for her."

Art nodded. "I will hold him in the Light."

A few sad tears left her eyes, and Helia wiped them.

"Art," Helene said, and when Art turned, Helene knelt beside her.

Art laid a shaky hand on Helene's shoulder and looked into
her eyes for haemorrhaging, caused by strangulation. She knew
Helene had breathed soundly even as she'd choked the blood
flow to her brain, but she had to make certain.

"You blood-choked me, Art," Helene said.

"Aye?" Art said. Helene's eyes appeared clear.

"I am never blood-choked," Helene said. "Ever."

She sat by Art and pulled the blankets around herself, then pressed close, warm and solid.

"Thee only napped," Art reassured, "with gentle snores."

"I do not snore."

"Thee did, into my mouth."

"Your mouth, what?" Helene said.

"Did thee dream?" Art said. She wanted to hug Helene to her. "Did thee frolic with tigers?"

"It was a white tiger. With blue eyes." Helene held up a steaming cup. "Here, Art. Drink this."

She put the cup to Art's lips and forestalled her remark. Art had a taste of the hot mixture before she could pull away.

"'Tis spirits!" she said in horror.

"Medicinal spirits, Art," Helene said cheerfully. She made Art drink more, silencing her. "Purl will warm you up quickly!"

"Hurrah!" Helia said. Somehow she'd obtained a cup of her own and held it up. "I have broken temperance as well! To dear Art, and to the defeat of the Frost Fair Ice Demon!"

"*Hurrah!*" cheered the butcher's people around them. They hoisted cups and cheered more.

"Ha-ha-ha," Art said. "Ha-ha-ha-ha!" Her cheeks felt hot, as did her belly, and she'd stopped shivering.

"That was quick," Helene said.

She made Art drink again.

"Oh dearest, you are inebriated!" Helia said, embracing Art's arm. "Don't worry. We'll never tell the Friends. Helene, her regenerative powers would make anything she ingests have immediate effect!"

"We'll leave smoking for another time, then," Helene said.

Helia sipped her own cup and gave a little shake at the liquor's strength. She laughed and held her drink up again. "And *this* is capable of wrecking the most stalwart of women!"

"*To Purl! Hurrah!*" the butcher's people cheered again. Someone shouted beyond the butcher's perimeter and musicians launched into a rousing number. Fairgoers began to dance.

Helene plucked Helia's cup from her grasp. Before she set it aside, she sniffed the contents, a wistful smile on her lips.

"You didn't drink much, did you?" Helene asked her sister.

"Only a taste to keep Art company," Helia said, hugging Art's arm.

"A good reason," Helene said. They watched the dancing that could be seen beyond the fences.

"Thee," Art said, poking Helene playfully beneath the blankets.

"Art?" Helene said, turning to her.

"Theeee," Art said, looking Helene in the eye. "Thee handed out strong meat today."

Helene gave her a questioning look.

"Thee knows how to fight me."

"I don't know what you mean, Art," Helene said.

"Ha-ha-ha," Art chuckled. She wagged a finger. "I know *now*, what thee knows, that I know . . . that thee knows. Thee has thought on how to defeat me."

"Nonsense, Art." Helene's cheeks reddened a little.

Art touched her nose. "Let thee try," she said.

Helene looked down. Her lips parted as if to say something. Instead, she reached beneath the blankets and found Art's aching thigh. She firmly rubbed the hurt muscles through Art's skirts and massaged the injury. Art sighed.

"Oh, that's—" She belched and covered her mouth in surprise.

Helene picked up the second cup.

"Drink more, Art," she encouraged.

Art did so, holding the cup. Helene returned her hands to her thigh. The soothing, firm touch was the last thing she remembered.

⤫

Art woke to a dull throb beating in her head and a tongue dry
and rough as a hairbrush. Her pained eye saw the dull glow of
sunlight on red wallpaper. She was lying in her own bed at the
Vesta.

"Good morning!" Jim said from her nightstand.

"Jim, not so loud," Art whimpered.

"Art, what a bleary face! Your feeble expression is forgiven,
for you were a roisterer of the first order last night, and what a
merry dancer you can be! Like a puppet with knotted strings!"

"I—what?" Art whispered.

"It was a night you'll never forget! The Ladies Skycourt, oh!
Revellers to behold, so gay on their feet! Lady Helia leapt like
she'd wings, and Lady Helene—so fast, so deft! I lost breath at
the sight of them. I could have watched all night, but thanks to
Delphia's light footwork, I too gave sprightly account."

"I recall nothing," Art said tearfully.

She tried sitting up. Both her pounding head and her nau-
seous stomach preferred she lie back down.

"I should mention that whilst we revelled, gladdened by
death averted, the *Terror* disappeared last night," Jim said.
"Sailed right out of the Port of London. It's gone. And no, it's
not our fault the Metropolitan Police couldn't keep the ship
from drifting. The Royal Geographical Society will have stern
words about that."

Art held her head and pondered that. She immediately dis-
carded the thought that Helene might have arranged the ship's
disappearance. She'd only had interest in the queer metal.

"And do you know what's interesting, Art? When Delphia
and I left to visit Scotland Yard—"

"What hour of the day is it now, Friend?" Art hoarsely exclaimed.

"It's nearly noon, young wastrel! You were snoring fit to shake the windowpanes. I hadn't the heart to wake you. Thus we left thee happily smacking thy lips and dreaming of kittens and pretty twins—"

"Jim," Art interrupted. "Thee spoke of Scotland Yard?"

She saw that a page had left food and drink on her table by the windows. A fresh trout had been laid on a bed of crisp ice, beside a pitcher of water.

Art held out her hand, and the water, ice, and trout flew across the room and into her body. She glowed and felt marginally less parched.

"Yes!" Jim said. "I thought I'd look upon those odd pieces of metal again, the ones hidden in Sir Baffin's cot. Just to indulge some professional curiosity. It seems the police never found the pieces. For all we know, they've sailed on with the *Terror*."

Art slowly nodded. Perhaps Helene had sent her man, Ganju Rana, to retrieve the fragments. Right after the agents left the ship.

"Heh-heh!" Jim chuckled. "Thus click the gears in thy tender head. But Art, you harboured the creature, and I wondered if you learned something of what it was."

"I might have, Friend," Art said. "I thought it a mermaid . . . but a mermaid not of our Earth."

"Ho?" Jim said. "*Ho?* You mean—? Hm! *Hurmm*. Well, now!"

"Aye. Now thy gears are clicking."

"Indeed! Indeed," Jim said in a hushed tone. "Extraordinary. In the interest of making certain this knowledge never leaves this room, let us speak no more of our ice-breathing friend, then. Especially where Dr Fall is concerned. We will write our reports accordingly. Note that I touch the side of my nonexistent nose."

"I note the touch, Friend."

"So!" he continued. "Our Frost Fair, Art! The Thames should

remain frozen a few days longer, and I've already acquired a treasure trove of souvenirs! I've an inscribed mug, and an engraved spoon, a lithograph, an illustrated book! Several poems, though one is a rather questionable limerick—"

Art cleared her throat.

"And what of John Rowden?" she queried.

"Ah." Jim paused. "Did you know his wife was a former songstress, Art? A brave woman. All night, she sang their favourite sea songs. No better earthly herald had a man, to usher his meeting with those who sing above."

Art nodded. She closed her eyes and gave prayer.

"But Art, the fair! After all your gay gyrations and admirable attempts at warbling, you purchased a most especial souvenir of your own!"

"I did?" Art wondered if she'd gotten a commemorative Frost Fair tattoo.

Jim hopped on the nightstand, and she noticed that he sat beside a propped-up cabinet card. It was from the photographer's tent at the fair. Art perched upon the giant moon crescent, the Skycourt twins on each knee as she embraced them both by the waist. Helene sat erect like a woman sidesaddle on a steed, chin raised and a hand on her hip, her mouth curling. Helia smiled warmly, and Art thought almost shyly, one gloved hand on Art's shoulder and the other clasping Art's hand at her waist. Art's own eyes were half-closed and her mouth slightly open, as if she were in the middle of a smile, a word, or a belch.

"Oh!" Art said. "I look the simpleton!"

"Yet such a lucky simpleton, with a lovely lady on each knee! You exclaimed all night that it was the happiest moment of your young Quaker life!"

Art made a rueful, affectionate sound as she looked at the photo. "How kind they are to disregard their respectability and indulge me."

She carefully embraced the card.

"Art!" Jim nearly shouted.

"Ohhh, Jim, please." Art held her head.

"I only want to show you your other gift! Courtesy of the ladies Skycourt!" He swivelled on the nightstand to regard a small parcel wrapped in blue paper that could fit Art's palm. She laid her card aside and picked the parcel up. Helia's handwriting was atop:

> Purchased this day, 27th of November, year 1880, at
> Frost Fair on the Thames for our beloved Artemis. With
> Love, Helia and Helene Skycourt.

Art carefully pulled up a corner of the folded paper. Within she saw gingerbread.

"Loves," she softly said.

❧

The winter being harsh, Art didn't think Helia should stay in her balloon replica home in the cold, Royal Aquarium any longer. Once she was dressed and less sickly of face, she visited Helia at her customary Blue Vanda table to tell her so.

Thus, by evening time they were both enjoying the warm stove in Helene's ascetic quarters in Whitechapel. Helene was not present, having departed for the Arctic that morning. Helia sat on Art's lap while Art watched her type, the typewriter standing atop several of Helene's books on the table. Pinned on Helene's sparse wall was a chart of Earth's farthest northern seas and continents. Cartography tools lay by Helia's typewriter with copied material from The Terror's logbook, relating the ship's charted course to the Arctic. Helia paused to search the table and then lift her typewriter to look at the book titles. She tutted.

"Oh! She took the nautical almanac with her," she said.

She resumed typing, and Art picked up a drafting compass.

"Helene likes her ships," Art said. "As we sit here, she may be, right now, sitting with the snow people, the Inuit?"

Helia nodded. "They've a story passed down, Art. It speaks of a fiery rock that fell from the sky."

"I hope thy sister returns before Christmas."

"She will, Art, mere days from now," Helia said, smiling. "Our airships are very fast. And perhaps she'll bring you a cunning Inuit trinket."

Art bounced Helia on her knee and made her laugh. While Helia typed more, Art looked at Helene's sea chart and pretended it was of the stars. Helene had also shared consciousness with the creature, and perhaps she better understood its true home than Art could hope to articulate. She would like to ask her.

"What if there had been another like Friend Baffin?" she said thoughtfully. "With a great ship, but one that explored amongst the heavenly spheres and happened upon an ocean; an ocean on an icy moon. And perhaps he, too, discovered a strange and beautiful creature in that water, and took it as a trophy to show his own circle."

Helene turned and touched Art's face. She kissed her on the cheek.

"And perhaps this explorer lost his ship as well, only it fell into our Earth, our Arctic," Art said.

She pondered more.

"It fell, because the mermaid caused that ship's failing too."

"Yes," Helia said, nodding in agreement.

"What shall thee call thy penny dread?" Art asked.

Helia pulled out her sheet from the typewriter and showed the manuscript's title to Art.

"*Diamond Breath*," Art read.

⚬

Near Norway, a sea storm raged, and in that churning ocean the *Terror* tossed. Great waves struck the deck. At the wheel stood a deck boy not more than twelve, an orphan of India who had cared for nothing except to escape home and see the world. London had been his port of call, and he'd been at sea since the age of nine. But the entity within him sensed that even the boy knew enough about the ship and storm that besieged them to fear that their vessel would not last longer. The boy looked up through the dark and rain and saw the lights of a hovering airship, beaten by the winds. A rope ladder dropped from it, bearing a large man on its rungs. He pointed a harpoon gun and fired, piercing the deck. With the ladder anchored and the gun secured to it, he jumped down to the rolling ship.

He was a great big African man, tall and wide of shoulders, even taller than the ghost woman. Both his hair and beard were in braids, and he wore the black dress coat of a captain. He looked down with dark, flashing eyes and thrust out his gloved hands. In both great fists he held a chart open and showed it to the boy. It displayed Earth, Saturn, and the stars.

"You who call yourself Diamond," he boomed above the roar of the winds. "I am Captain Taurus Midas Kingdom, and you will come with me! We who serve Lady Helene Skycourt will take you to your second home, the Arctic. But this she promises you, as heir to the earldom of Skycourt and of its ships: for as long as it takes, we will learn how to fly you back to the stars and to your true home!"

The boy let go of the wheel and held up his arms. The man snatched him up as the deck tilted. He grabbed for the ladder.

He released the harpoon anchor, and they flew up through the whipping winds for the airship and the black sky above.

The end.

Character Key
Author's Notes
A glimpse into Dark Victorian: BONES

Character Key
(in order of appearance):

Mrs Genevieve Rowden (formerly Genny Tilly)
Lady Gertrude Baffin
John Rowden (helmsman of the SS Terror)
Sir Francis Baffin (polar explorer)
Captain Buckamore (captain of the SS Terror)
Artifice (also known as Artemis)
Jim Dastard
Miss Delphia Bloom
Sgt Barkley of the Metropolitan Police
Lady Helia Skycourt (journalist for the Times)
Lady Helene Skycourt
Miss Aldosia Stropps (illustrator for the Strand)
Mrs Farney (maid to Mr and Mrs Rowden)
Miss Wila Stanchfield (the other woman illustrator for the
Strand)
Diamond
Captain Taurus Midas Kingdom

Author Notes:

Timeline:
Ice Demon occurs in November of the year 1880 and after the stories in Risen and Bones, which happen in March.

The SS Terror:
The SS Terror is not a true ship, but it is based on the HMS Terror, a British Royal Navy bomb-ship that was lost on an Arctic expedition:
www.ncbi.nlm.nih.gov/pmc/articles/PMC1279489/

The sea chanty, *The Lass That Loves a Sailor*:
I wanted a brass band present at the opening scene and needed to know what they played. It had to be something that a woman would want her husband to hear, and therefore probably not a carol, anthem, or military song—thus a sea chanty. Thankfully, I found *The Lass That Loves a Sailor*, composed by Charles Dibdin (1740–1814) and not to be confused with Gilbert & Sullivan's *HMS Pinafore*. Though the song's significance could be understood by the title alone, I thought a character ought to sing some of the lyrics, and when I chose Lady Baffin's companion to do it, suddenly Genevieve and John Rowden's love was put into greater clarity, one that became paralleled in Art's relationship with Helia and Helene. What's purely coincidence on my part is that the song was also referred to in James Joyce's *Dubliners* short story, *Eveline*. A midi file can be heard here:
http://www.james-joyce-music.com/extras/lasslovesailor.html

And there's a lovely version sung by the tenor Kevin McDermott and accompanied by pianist Ralph Richey on the album, *More Music from the Works of James Joyce*. You can search the song on YouTube and find at least two folksy renditions with voices of character.

When Jim says *Hokahey*:
Hokahey is Sioux for "Let's do it!" or "Let's go!" and is attributed to Lakota Sioux leader Crazy Horse, who said: "*Hokahey*! Today is a good day to die!"
http://www.native-languages.org/iaq21.htm

The Paraffin Blow Lamp:
How to play with your antique, brass paraffin blow lamp. This YouTube video is a fun reference:
http://youtu.be/3lLKs0ITZTE

Ice Fog, Sea Smoke, and Diamond Dust:
Meteorologists may quibble at my use of the term "ice fog", when I may be describing "freezing fog". Sea smoke, as mentioned by Lady Baffin, is fog formed over the sea.
I thought to distinguish the fog-like presence of the ice entity, Diamond, from common ice fog by having her resemble the phenomenon known as poconip/pogonip (a term attributed to the Shoshone tribe), or "diamond dust", where ice crystals are suspended in the fog and flash in sunlight. I'm uncertain if diamond dust really exists because I've yet to come across a scientific account that explains it (rather than one on the web based on hearsay), but here's a beautiful video showing it. If it's a digitally enhanced video, I can't tell:
http://youtu.be/Aq-BsY_0oz0

The blood choke and pressure points fighting:
The "blood choke", or the proper term, the "rear naked choke"

(RNC), is a martial arts technique and should only be executed with proper instruction from a qualified and trained teacher.

Fight Science MMA, Rear Naked Choke:
http://youtu.be/ovb6ZAOJ8mg

That also goes for pressure points fighting, which is pretty devastating stuff. I'm not a practitioner, so I'm only approximating Helene's nerve strikes (and let's face it, I'm deliberately approximating them because it is devastating stuff). That said, I highly encourage everyone to go to a dojo or class and learn even a little self-defence, no matter how old, young, or physically inept we may feel. It's good exercise, adds to body awareness and confidence, and teaches us what hurts and what works. Knowledge is power.

～

ELIZABETH WATASIN

The DARK
VICTORIAN

BONES

✿

A Glimpse Into:

Dark Victorian: BONES

"I Am Made Of This"

Chapter One

A heavy fog rolled through London. Gaslights broke the dark as a hackney carriage drove down a deserted, cobbled street. Inside the carriage, Inspector Risk, a tall, dark-haired man with a thick moustache, sat and grimly regarded Dr. Speller, a bespectacled man with white mutton chop sideburns seated across from him. Dr. Speller moved his top hat around in his hands in excitement. The plainclothes sergeant, Barkley, took notes.

"It's Esther Stubbings, I'm sure of it," Dr. Speller said. "She is one of your victims."

"I've four bodies," Risk said. "Just skin and muscle. Full skeletons and organs entirely removed and no incisions made. Makes it hard to identify flattened faces. You're claiming that the organ almost sold to you tonight belonged to this Esther Stubbings, and therefore she's my victim."

"Well I've yet to identify the body, but the organ is unquestionably hers, Inspector, because I was the surgeon," Speller said. "Every woman's reproductive organs are different. I mean in shape. I recognized my own work, sir; I was the one who removed her second ovary. And Esther was alive and well just last week. The only way someone could harvest her organs is if she were murdered."

"And since we've her female vitals she has been," Risk said. "So this organ stealer, knowing you were a women's physician and vivisectionist; he comes to you for a sale."

"I vivisected only to learn," Speller said. "But for the most part I now merely dissect organs purchased solely from the Royal Surgical Sciences Academy."

"Yes. The Academy. Who buys from men like the one you met tonight," Risk said. "Except this one knows to bring it directly to you. The dead woman I have is of the poor. We know it from her clothes. How can someone like that afford your services?"

"She can when she volunteers for the procedure," Speller said. "Like all members of the Academy I'm a man of science and medicine. Not only do I use the skills learned, I practice new techniques that have successfully corrected female ailments. Esther Stubbings was on her way to becoming a fully healthy woman. And none of it, thankfully, by use of supernatural nonsense, claiming healing through organ transference and such!"

"But that's exactly what I have, doctor," Risk said. "Black arts surgery. Unless you can explain how four people have no skulls, eyes, or brains in their intact heads unless it was all pulled out of their nostrils."

"Not to mention," Sergeant Barkley said. "How His Royal Highness can be here with us today if not for supernatural medicine. Been nineteen years since he nearly died! We've a bunch of nonsense to thank."

Risk sighed while Speller glowered. The carriage came to a halt outside a lit station house.

"You stay here," Risk said to Speller. "We'll move on to the mortuary shortly for you to identify the woman. And you," he said to Barkley. "Stop talking. Let's go."

When Risk stepped down from the carriage he saw a young woman in an azure coat briskly leave the station entrance. Her brown hat was crooked and wisps of dark hair escaped. Her skirts were cut high enough for the ankles of her boots to show. She wore a fitted leather mask on one side of her face. Helia Skycourt smiled at Risk and waved. She grabbed the penny-farthing resting against the station wall, took a running jump into the sidesaddle seat, and hit the treadle. The lantern in front of her wheel suddenly lit. She sped away into the dark and fog.

Risk watched her depart, incredulous.

"Damn journalist," he said. "Does she never sleep?" Barkley stifled a yawn. They entered the station building.

"Inspector," Barkley said in a low voice as they walked into the dimly lit room. A uniformed man was behind the desk. "This case . . . it being supernatural. When will the Secret Commission start helping?"

"When we ask for it," Risk said curtly. "And not before. What do you have?" he said to the policeman who rose to greet him.

"Sir," the policeman said. He led them down a narrow hall. "The fellow Dr. Speller had us arrest will be brought out of his cell shortly. He refuses to speak and has answered no questions. The doctor told us the man only spoke once during the negotiating of the price of the organ and his accent was German."

"Looks a foreigner, then?" Risk asked. He followed the policeman into a room with a desk and chairs. He took the seat behind the desk while Barkley went to stand near the small, barred window.

"No sir," the policeman answered. "Well dressed, clean-faced, trimmed hair, tidy, hands that haven't seen hard labor. I'm guessing he's of the medical profession."

"Organ stealers usually are," Risk said. "Especially those who work in mortuaries." They heard shuffling steps approach. Two policemen brought a shackled man into the room. He was a slim fellow, tight-lipped and with one, nervous eye. His other eye was removed, leaving a gaping, black socket. He did not bother to shut his eyelid. The men escorting him sat him in front of Risk.

"*Wie ist dein name?*" Risk said.

The man looked at him in surprise.

"The sooner you answer our questions," Risk said.."The sooner we catch who's doing these black arts surgeries. Because it isn't you, is it? So if you don't want the blame, give us some-one else's name."

The man's posture became stiffer.

"That's four dead," Risk said staring into the man's one eye. "Is the gallows worth this surgeon? Give him up and you won't have to worry. Do your sentence and then get on with life, right?"

Risk watched the man; the prisoner seemed to grow even more frightened.

"Right," Risk said slowly. "Now who is he?"

A shot exploded, shattering the window behind the sergeant. Blood sprayed into Risk's face. The other men shouted and ran out the door. The prisoner sat slumped. Brain matter hung from the side of his forehead where the exiting bullet had shattered the skull.

Shouts and running came from outside the station. Risk didn't bother looking out the broken window, knowing that all he'd see would be darkness and fog. He grimly pulled out his handkerchief and slowly wiped his face. Barkley touched the prisoner to see if he was still alive.

"Shall I send a message to the Secret Commission?" Barkley asked.

Risk stared at the dead man who'd just brought him an internal affairs nightmare.

"Do it," Risk said.

Read more in
Elizabeth Watasin's
Dark Victorian: BONES

The Author would like to Thank:

Phatpuppy Creations
phatpuppyart.com

Cover model, Elizabeth Worth
www.modelmayhem.com/3122503

Cavalyn Galano
for Custom Wardrobe Creation
www.facebook.com/CavalynDesign

Nadya Rutman for Makeup/Hair
www.bynadya.com

and

Teresa Yeh Photography
www.teresayeh.com

KEEP
CALM
GHOST
AND
SKULL
ARE
HERE

About The Author

Elizabeth Watasin is the acclaimed author of the Gothic steampunk series *The Dark Victorian*, The *Elle Black Penny Dreads*, and the creator/artist of the indie comics series *Charm School*, which was nominated for a Gaylactic Spectrum Award. A twenty year veteran of animation and comics, her credits include thirteen feature films, such as *Beauty and the Beast, Aladdin, The Lion King*, and *The Princess and the Frog*, and writing for *Disney Adventures* magazine. She lives in Los Angeles with her black cat named Draw, busy bringing readers uncanny heroines in shilling shockers, preternatural fantasies, and adventuress tales.

Follow the news of her latest projects at A-Girl Studio.
www.a-girlstudio.com
amazon.com/author/elizabethwatasin
www.facebook.com/ElizabethWatasinX
twitter.com/ewatasin

Look for more of Elizabeth's gothic tales in The Dark Victorian series:
RISEN, BONES, and EVERLIFE.

Made in the USA
Middletown, DE
30 July 2018